THE SIREN SERIES

Siren's Test

USA TODAY BESTSELLING AUTHOR
JESSICA CAGE

2

Written by Jessica Cage

Edited by Debbi Watson

Cover design by Solidarity Graphics

Book design by Jessica Cage

Printed in the United States of America

First Printing: April 2015

ISBN-13: 978-1-7364885-6-0

AUTOGRAPH PAGE

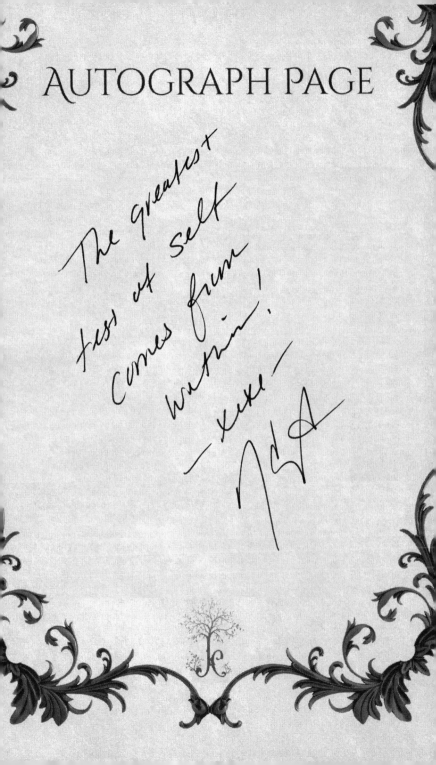

The greatest test of self comes from within!

-xoxo-

Contents

DEDICATION

To the dreamers and
those who wish for
something more.
Enjoy your life and make
every day the best it can
be!

PROLOGUE

L ife on land had become a nightmare and there was nothing I wanted more than to escape. I wanted to be free of being a hybrid of a siren and a witch that was currently being hunted by a coven of witches and other unknown beings. I wanted to run from the idea that my family was so fucked up, and that my own aunt was the reason my life had been thrown into complete chaos.

Even with my desire to flee my life, I couldn't help looking back as I swam into the light of the barrier between the human and siren worlds. Who knew what insanity waited for me on the other side?

Still, my red tail with the hypnotic gold spiral pushed me forward. The initial feeling was an intense warmth as the emerald rays of light tinted my arms and hands green. What followed that was a tingle of electricity accompanied by the sound of sparks. I tried to find Malachi's face and hoped for eye contact to give me a sense of reassurance, but the light was too bright.

All I could do was squeeze his hand even tighter and hope that he didn't let me go. The heat intensified for just a few moments longer before it cooled. The difference was undeniable once we crossed over the barrier. We came through the other side into an open mass of water that was as clear as the air I once walked through in the human realm, and even felt a cool breeze as it moved across the skin.

My body was lighter in this realm. I hadn't realized how much effort it took to push my body through the water before. Once we crossed over, I felt as though I was moving without even a thought about the action. It was just like Tylia, my siren tutor, had described.

"This is awesome!" I spoke and my mouth moved to emit the sound. "What the hell? I thought we could only speak with our minds while underwater?" I looked at Malachi, who smiled.

"That rule only applies in the human realm. Here the water is different. We are different. On this side of the barrier the water is like air. We breathe it and it nourishes our bodies," Malachi spoke as he swam ahead. His tail brushed against my own and sent a trembling response along the length of it.

"Well, that is pretty badass. At least now I don't have to worry about choking." I laughed and swam around a bit, enjoying the airy feeling of the water. I knew it was there, but I couldn't feel it. It was pure and didn't sit on the skin like the water we had just left.

Demetrius, my second guardian, said something to Malachi that I didn't catch and then swam ahead. I watched him leave; the strength of his muscles as he moved was fascinating. A strong solid man above a deep blue tail, which stood in contrast to the rich golden hues of his brother's.

He refused eye contact with me, and I would not force any connection to happen. Our relationship was in a tough place. We would have time to talk things out once we arrived wherever they had deemed safe for us to be. I still did not know where that was, but there was no turning back now.

I noted the surrounding beauty as well. The reef that filled the space below us was a rainbow of colors. The small ecosystem was teeming with life. I could hear them, and it was all so clear, the chatter of the animals that dwelled along its surface. They were all so happy and the sound made me feel a bit more relaxed and confident in my decision to follow my leaders.

I should have known it wouldn't last. Moments later, Demetrius, brother of Malachi and my second protector, came hurrying over the reef, yelling to us they were coming and that we needed to take cover.

It was a total ambush. It seemed completely unreal, but the second we crossed that barrier, our enemy was alerted, and they quickly responded. I had exactly four seconds to relish in the beauty of this new world before they struck. At least thirty Mermen attacked us, launching nets and spears.

Malachi and Demetrius fought them off for as long as they could, but there were just too many of them and my defenders were weaponless. The only ammo we had was whatever we could scavenge. This equated to rocks and eventually the weapons we could snatch from our attackers.

I tried to help them, and I did for a while. I had just pulled a man off Demetrius' back when another man grabbed by tail and flung into the side of the reef. My head smacked the surface and my vision blurred as my ears filled with the sound of the tiny inhabitants' screams.

The impact of my head against the hard surface left me confused. It took a while for the effect to wear off, but I could still make out what was happening around me. Malachi shouted with elation that help had arrived, and the men he referred to appeared over a reef and quickly worked against our opponents.

The youngest brother continued fighting. But I couldn't see or hear Demetrius. My vision cleared just in time to watch a spear pierce Demetrius' body, and his blood seep out into the water. I screamed out his name at the same moment that Malachi rushed over to his dying brother.

He ripped the charm from his neck, and it looked as if he would use it to plug the hole in his brothers' belly when a burly man punched Malachi in the side of his head. Malachi shook off the effects of the punch, elbowed the man in the throat and in a swift moment wrapped his arm around his neck. With a quick jerk, he snapped the man's neck.

Malachi tried to recover his brother, but he was too late. Demetrius' body sunk to the ocean floor as Malachi, who held the charm clutched in his hand, screamed out for his brother.

Malachi's name ripped through the water from my own mouth. The pain in my body vanished when I witnessed what happened. I needed to get to them; I needed to help them. He, Malachi, could never survive the loss of his brother. He already held on to so much guilt. I had to help him, but it was already too late. I never even made it to Malachi.

A large pair of arms wrapped around my waist, and I was being tugged away from him as a deep voice murmured in my ear. Something about getting to safety. A similar set of arms carried my grief-stricken friend as well. Our saviors towed us away just in time.

Large creatures that looked like sharks, but twice as large as any I'd ever known of and each with a pair of spiked tentacles, flooded the battlefield and in moments they disappeared, leaving behind not even a bone as evidence of the fight. I tried to see if Demetrius' body was still there, but I couldn't tell. I prayed like hell that one of our heroes had thought to save his body from the hungry beasts.

CHAPTER I

"*M* *alachi?" My knuckles tapped lightly* on a door made of a material that closely resembled a fusion of wood and metal. Though it had only been a few days, it felt like an eternity had passed since they separated me from Malachi.

An overbearing woman named Chaney scolded me whenever I asked about him. She said he needed his time alone and implied that my presence would only make matters worse for him. Against her orders and with some ingenuity, I'd escaped confinement and found my way to his room.

It wasn't hard to do. They had us in the underwater tower which in the days since my arrival had been practically abandoned. The merpeople didn't keep their skepticism secret. They didn't know me and didn't want to be near me.

I knocked again, hoping for a response, but there was nothing. Hearing the approaching chatter of two women, I panicked. With no invitation, I entered the room. The door shut behind me just as the pair of sirens turned the corner. I pressed my ear against the door, listening until they were out of earshot. I relaxed, took a deep breath, and turned to press my back against the door.

Everything else in the underwater structure glowed with an unnatural light, while Malachi's domicile was completely pitch-black. It was like something had completely snuffed the magical element out. I called to him again, feeling his presence in the room, but he didn't respond. I could hear him breathing and feel the weight of his eyes. His perception of me left a trail of heat across my body.

"Are you okay?" I spoke to hear my own voice more than to gain his response. My stomach turned as I floated forward. "Malachi?" I called his name again. "I can feel you here. Please answer me."

"What are you doing here?" His voice was low and sinister and completely broken.

"I wanted to see you." I moved further into the darkness and a new physical weight drug me down.

The tip of my tail rubbed across the floor as I tried to remain upright. It felt like swimming in the waters of the human realm. In this world, the water was like air. But when we crossed the barrier, you could feel the weight of it against your skin and it you had to work harder to keep your tail moving.

What caused that effect? Was it him?

"I told them to keep you away." His words plunged into my chest like a dagger. It wasn't Chaney who kept us apart. This was his wish.

Why would he want us to be separated?

"Yes, I know." I lied because I didn't want him to know that his choice hurt me. It was better if he thought that this was another case of me just being hard-headed. It wasn't the first time I had gone against his wishes, so it wouldn't be too difficult for him to believe.

"Why can't you ever do as I ask?" There was a slight tone of humor, not much, but enough to give me hope for the hidden man.

"Why would you ever expect me to when it is not what I want?" I moved forward, using the sound of his voice for guidance.

"You have to be smarter than this!" His growl vibrated the water and I paused.

If I had any sense or concern for self-preservation, I might have turned back. Knowing that Malachi was an angry half demon cloaked in darkness should have been enough to inspire me to be more cautious. It wasn't. All I knew was that I was in a new world, and he was the only person I trusted. I'd seen him at his worst. How bad could this possibly be?

"Smarter than what?" I reached out into the darkness, hoping to find him with my hands. "You're my friend and you're hurting. I want to be here for you, to help you."

How could he expect anything else from me? Did he honestly believe that I would ever be able to just turn and walk away from him?

"You can't help me, Sy." I was close enough to feel the change in the water as he moved.

"And why not?" I pushed deeper into the darkness.

"Stop." Malachi warned. "Sy, you need to turn back."

"Why are you hiding from me?" I reached out again and felt the water shift as he moved away from me. "Malachi, I want to be here for you."

"You really need to go." Something sinister, bubbling beneath the surface, made his voice tremble.

"Malachi," I cut my protest short when two glowing orbs appeared before me.

I blinked to clear my vision. Were my eyes playing tricks on me?

The orbs moved side to side, then vanished, but quickly returned. I reached out again, this time making contact. A soft gasp escaped me as I realized what I was touching. My finger stroked the tip of his nose and he blinked again, disrupting the soft red light. Malachi's eyes glowed like embers in a flame.

"I," Suddenly I wanted to heed his warning and escape the room, but I couldn't.

My tail felt heavier than it ever had, and when I tried to push myself back through the water, my entire body seized. His gaze held me captive. The longer I stared into his eyes, the hotter I became. And that heat spread from my face, across my body.

Beads of sweat hung to my flesh, despite the surrounding water. The fire reached my stomach, and I felt like I would vomit. I didn't think it could get worse, but it did. As it moved lower, my tail reacted. Red and gold scales unraveled, and my lower half shifted from tail to legs.

"What the hell?" I panicked, kicking my legs beneath me. The fear that I would start drowning without my tail caused me to hyperventilate.

"Sy, stop. Calm down." Malachi spoke.

"What is this? How is this possible?" I flailed around like a toddler tossed in the deep end.

"I don't know." Malachi walked forward and with each step came a dim glow of red that allowed me to see him. "The only other person I've ever seen walk on legs underwater was Demetrius."

He wasn't the man I knew, but the side of him I'd only seen once before. Standing before me was the monster, his demon. Just as before, the transformation had distorted his face and his body was twice the size. Malachi was completely naked. The glow of red beneath his flesh highlighted the enhanced muscles. The transformation was a strain on his body, making him look more like a bodybuilder, permanently flexing for show.

I stood there like stone as he circled me. I followed him with my eyes until he disappeared behind me. I couldn't see him, but I could feel him. He pressed his chest against my back, and the warmth of his breath brushed against my right cheek.

When his hand caressed my thigh, I moaned and leaned back into him. There was no controlling my siren this time. The moment he touched me, she came to life and called out to him. As his fingers moved up my thigh, my soft moan turned into a quiet siren song.

"Sy." He growled in my ear and the vibration shot down to my throbbing center.

"Yes?" Voice trembling, I sought his face again as he moved to stand in front of me.

"You're mine." Malachi declared, claiming his territory in the most primal way as he moved in front of me.

He grabbed me, lifting me to wrap my legs around his waist. Our lips met, and he kissed me with such aggression I could barely breathe. His hand reached under the shirt I wore and ripped away my bra. So much for decency beneath the sea.

"Malachi." I moaned his name as his fingers pinched my nipple.

"You belong to me, Syrinada." He spoke in a low growl that frightened me.

A logical mind would have told me to pull away from him. Logic was the furthest thing from my mind. Passionate hunger was my driving force. Instinctively, my arms wrapped around his neck as I pressed myself against his body. I still couldn't bring myself to promise him this bond, but I needed him in a way I hadn't realized.

Malachi gripped my waist and waited for my response. I knew what he wanted. Confirmation of his claim. But if I said it, it would be a lie. Instead of proclaiming a connection I did not want, I kissed him and pushed my hips against him. He resisted me at first, holding out for what he wanted. But when I bit down on his shoulder, he gave in.

He lifted my ass with one hand, and with the other he grabbed himself and found my opening. My back arched as he entered me. My eyes bulged as I realize that with his transformation, *every* part of him expanded. I bit my lip and gasped as my walls stretched to fit him.

His first entry was slow, testing my capacity to receive him. My arms wrapped around his neck as he moved in and out of me, each thrust reaching deeper than the one before it. He continued the pace, slow and steady, until my first orgasm.

"Fuck!" He groaned and gripped my ass. His nails digging into my flesh.

"What's wrong?" I asked, my hips still shaking from my climax.

"I want you," He growled tightening his hold on me.

"I'm here." I looked him in the eyes and saw what he really meant. Malachi was holding back. "Fuck me."

"Sy, I don't want to hurt you."

I jumped down from his arms, turned my back to him, and bent over. Ass in the air, I grabbed his dick and slid the head inside my pussy.

"I said, fuck me, Malachi." I repeated.

With a devious grin, he grabbed my waist and gave me all that he had. That first thrust was so powerful I nearly reconsidered, but I held my own. Malachi folded me over completely and I gripped my ankles as he did exactly as I asked. He pounded my pussy until I came again.

But he wasn't done with me. As soon as the orgasm finished, he lifted me to his shoulder and buried his face between my legs. Malachi ate my pussy like he'd missed a month of meals. I smacked the ceiling with my hands as I felt another climax building.

He stopped just before it hit, lowered me from his face, and as he kissed me, his dick slid back into me. I drug my nails across his skin, trying not to cum until he wanted me to.

"Oh, shit." I moaned.

"Sy," Malachi was near his breaking point.

"Malachi." I wrapped my arms around his head, shoving his face to my breast.

"Come with me, baby." He wrapped his hand in my hair and pulled my head back.

He bit my neck, and the sensation shattered any control I had. I called out his name with my orgasm and felt him erupt within me.

When Malachi finished, the light had returned to the interior of the room. His body calmed and though he was still throbbing inside of me, his temperature lowered. He returned the spelled charm around his neck before he went to the task of kissing my breast and nibbling on my nipples.

Within seconds, my Malachi, the one I'd known for years, returned.

"I want you like this." he said in a husky voice.

"Yes." I kissed him and again he took me.

Malachi pressed his body against mine lifting my leg so he could slide inside of me. We rocked together until again we reached the peak together.

After my body finished trembling, Malachi lowered me back to my feet. Once we separated, the water in the room moved, like being stirred by a spoon. That heavy feeling eased, and the beautiful crimson tail with golden spiked replaced his legs. I watched him, but I felt my body change. When I looked down, my tail, which matched his gold and red hues, reformed beneath me.

"That was intense." I looked around, hoping the bra he ripped from me was still salvageable. It was not.

"Yeah, it was." Malachi looked down at his tail as if surprised to find it there.

"What happens now?" I asked, but he was too busy assessing himself. "Are you okay?"

Would he ever truly be okay again? After three searches, they still hadn't found his brother. Demetrius took a fatal hit when opposing Mermen ambushed us as we crossed from the human realm. Unfortunately, we lost sight of him as we fled.

I thought about asking Malachi about his brother. To see how he was handling the loss. But it felt weird after what we'd just done. Because though we never acted on it, there was something between Demetrius and I. Would my concern for the lost brother cause Malachi to doubt me. Would he even want to discuss it? What if talking about Demetrius brought his demon back to the surface?

"Yes." he nodded and for a moment I thought he would approach the topic I agonized over. He did not.. "Now, you will do what you came here to do. Go get your Siren stone."

Malachi spoke of the symbol of power which every siren hoped to gain. At least every siren who grew up knowing what the hell it was. I hadn't. I grew up on land, a supposed orphan and the furthest things from my bucket list was traveling through a mystical passageway to prove myself worthy of some great power.

That's what I had to do, though. Because regardless of what I wanted for myself there were people who would force my hand. People who thought I was dangerous simply because I existed and who threatened to kill me. It was because of those people that I felt like Alice, headed down the rabbit hole.

"Okay, so how do we get there?" I perked up. Finally, we could do more than just sit around waiting for meals to be delivered. Underwater living wasn't as enjoyable as I hoped it would be. The sooner I got my stone, the sooner I could get back to life on land.

"I won't be going with you, Sy." He shook his head. "It's just going to be you. This is something you have to do without me."

"Wait, how am I supposed to do this by myself?" My stomach clenched with worry. "I mean, I barely know anything about this place. Most of the people here don't want me here and now I'm supposed to go searching the seas alone?"

"You will be fine. You've already proven your strength and your power. Now is the time to put those two things to use." Malachi had faith in me, a blind faith that was not mirrored by my own feelings. "And no one is going to mess with you. They aren't that dumb."

"Tell that to the men who attacked us when we got here." I spat and then blushed because I realized I'd done exactly what

I wanted to avoid. Malachi frowned, no doubt recollecting the attack that resulted in his brother's demise.

"Sy," He sighed.

"But, I thought you would go with me." I frowned. "You're going to have to forgive me for being upset right now, but you said we were in this together and now you're telling me I'm on my own."

"The rules do not allow mermen to travel the passage of the stone. They will assign you a guide. Another siren who will assist you, but she too can only go so far. Your journey is your own, Sy. You will have help along the way, but the result, whether you succeed or not, is entirely up to you."

"Why didn't you tell me all of this before?" I rolled my eyes, unable to hide my frustration.

"Would you have come if you'd known?" He challenged with a smile.

"Maybe," I crossed my arms over my chest and turned my back to him.

"Yeah. Right." He chuckled and my stomach filled with butterflies.

CHAPTER 2

I stayed in his room that night. Malachi was still distant as he processed the loss of his brother, but he was there with me. Instead of talking about his feelings, he told me more about the sea. The magical properties that made it possible for us to talk, and of the creatures that existed within it.

The waters were called Deuterio. Where the human waters had many names, the Siren waters had one. Within Deuterio were many underwater cities inhabited by our people. And you could tell where a siren was from based on their accessories, body mass, and even hairstyles.

The people of Mioku wore long braids decorated with seashells, while those from Vunar chopped their hair off. Their city sat closer to the surface of the Deuterio making the waters warmer. Hair to them was more of a hassle than anything.

Despite his explanation of these people, his attempt to make them more relatable, I felt no connection. They didn't feel like they belonged to me, and I expressed that to him openly.

"I know this is supposed to feel like home, but it doesn't." I laced my fingers with his as we float side by side beneath the blanket. "I was really hoping to feel connected to this place."

It was odd, but even underwater, we slept on a bed beneath a blanket. The only difference was the blanket had to be tied down to keep it from floating away. It kept the body warm while sleeping. When a siren slept, their body temperature plummeted. If it dropped too low, they would die. They made the blankets with a special fiber that recycled the escaping body heat and fed it back into the person. The first two nights there, I couldn't sleep for fear of the damn thing malfunctioning.

"Give it time. Soon you'll know this place like the back of your hand, and you'll feel right at home."

We were in Xylon. It was the home of some of their most powerful elders. And their presence was the only reason I was still alive. Not everyone in Xylon agreed with my being there, but they respected the elders and would not defy their wishes.

The ones who had attacked us were from a neighboring city called Skynar. They had no such respect for the elders. Fear ruled them and a hybrid siren who the covens of earth wanted dead was something that terrified them. Their solution was to take out the problem before it unfolds.

"Why was I able to have my legs before?" The question had been looming in my mind for hours.

"I don't know. Like I said, the only other person I've ever seen do that is my brother. Most Mer-people only have their tails underwater. Humans who were lured to the water by sires kept their legs, but they die quickly." He scratched his chin as he contemplated the conundrum. "Witches are different. They have their own magic. They use their power to create air pockets so they can breathe. My father is the reason I can do it. My guess is it's the same for you."

"Oh." I didn't go any further with my questions. Tylia, Malachi's informally adopted mother, told me about his parents. His mother, the siren, his father, the demon. Malachi's background was just as messed up as my own, if not more so.

Eventually we slept. Malachi held me close to him the entire night. Every time I moved, his arm tightened around my waist and pulled me back into him. I didn't mind it. It was the first time I spent the night in bed with a man. Yeah, lame, I know, but I'd never had a sleepover before.

I was happy to have a moment that felt so normal. Late night talk, exhausting sex, and cuddles. That's what every girl wanted. Or at least that's what I wanted. Yes, it was underwater. Yes, it was the night before I would have to face a city of people who hated me, but it was nice. It was also the first night since being there that I didn't have nightmares.

As the light returned to the water, signifying daybreak, Malachi woke me. Soft kisses on my cheek pulled me from a dream about sex and cheesecake.

"Wake up, Sy," He shook my shoulder and kissed my cheek again.

"A few more minutes, please." I pushed my ass against his lap, hoping to persuade him.

He groaned. "Alright now, you're going to start something doing that."

"Maybe I want to start something." I smirked, refusing to open my eyes. If I opened them, I'd be accepting defeat and would have to wake up.

"As much as I would love that." he pushed his hips forward, teasing me. "We have to go. They're going to announce who your guide will be today."

Malachi wanted me to be excited, but it was difficult to inspire enthusiasm when he clearly had his own doubts.

"Today? Why so soon?" I hadn't even had time to see this new world, and already they were kicking me out. I'd spent days just trying to get back to him.

"Sorry, Sy, but having you here is a risk. If you can't protect yourself and help to protect our people, which without your stone, you cannot do, they will want you to leave." There was the harsh slap of reality I'd been waiting for. I was unwanted, unless useful.

"I guess it was pretty foolish to expect any kind of warm welcome from them. Half of these people want me dead, right?"

"Maybe a little more than half." he nudged my shoulder and released the blanket lock. It floated to the ceiling above us.

"Ah, great." I clapped and shifted to an upright position. "Bring it on!" Fake it until you make it. It wasn't the best tactic, but at that moment, it was all I had.

Traveling through the underwater city with Malachi was the first time I had been outside since arriving in Xylon. No one forced me to remain inside, but I didn't want to leave without him. I was in a foreign place surrounded by things that I didn't understand. I needed Malachi by my side.

Xylon was beautiful. The underwater city reminded me of my hometown Chicago. Tall buildings, architectural works of art, lined the streets. Reaching up to the surface of the water and fixed with massive windows, all capable of opening. The buildings didn't have stairs, but there were hallways and passageways that connected the floors. Most people swam in and out of the structure through the windows, though each building had doors on the bottom level.

As nervous as I was, it was amazing to see the people living their lives. Swimming in and out of buildings and going about their days. Conversations, laughter, disagreements, the sounds of life. It was all so normal and yet so strange.

For the first few minutes, I was a spectator in this new world, but soon I became the spectacle. The unfamiliar siren, with the strange tail, swimming besides the alpha who hadn't been home in years. Eyes locked on us, fingers pointed in our direction, and whispers carried across the current. They wondered who I was and what the hell I was doing there.

A small child swam toward me as she exclaimed how pretty my tail was. I smiled at her, but that expression was quickly slapped from my face as her mother pulled her back and refused to let her get anywhere near me.

It was just as uncomfortable for Malachi. Women eyed Malachi as if the devil himself had come to town. Men acted as though they needed to defend the others from him. I looked to my protector who moved forward, head high, as if he had noticed none of it. In that moment, I took a lesson from him and refused to let the attitudes of others affect the way I handled myself.

"It's her," I said as we moved through a crowd of merpeople who parted like the red sea as we passed.

"Who?" he asked.

"The siren I told you about in New Orleans. Verena." I pointed the auburn-haired siren out in the crowd.

Verena had that kind of vibrancy about her you just couldn't miss. Her smile was wide, and her eyes told a story you'd begged to hear. Under the water, her skin looked brighter, and her aura lured in the surrounding men. I remembered my lessons with Tylia, the woman who taught me to control my pull. Verena was an expert. She directed her energy in targets, hitting one man, skipping two, and snagging the fourth. Only those she wanted would ever experience her draw.

"What is she doing here?" I asked Malachi.

"No Idea. People come and go as they please." He shrugged and caught sight of someone I assumed was a friend. "Wait here I'll be right back."

He stepped away to meet his friend, leaving me alone and vulnerable. I wanted to sink beneath the ocean floor and stay there until he returned. Passing men looked at me with a mixture of desire and disgust. The women still pointed and whispered what I imagined being horrible things about me. I wanted to run but kept my head high and waited for Malachi to return.

"Syrinada!" Verena swam over to me. I wasn't sure if talking to her would be a good idea, but it was better than standing there alone.

"What are you doing here?" I asked as her arms crushed me in a hug that I gave no consent to.

Verena clearly had no concern for what people thought of her. Those same people who were just staring at her with desire turned their noses up in disgust when she embraced me.

"Well, I should ask you that, newbie. I should also ask you what you are doing with such a hunk of a merman." She winked at Malachi, and I felt something strange and territorial stirring inside of me.

"It was an apparent necessity." I attempted to hide my discomfort but could tell that I failed by the uneasy look she gave in return.

"I see, well those higher up the food chain summoned me. And of course, they didn't give me a reason. Either way, I am just thrilled to be seeing you again after your vanishing act. We barely got to have any girl talk!" She clapped her hands. "I had so many questions for you, girl. And I'm sure with you being a newcomer, you have things you would like to ask me. I can help you navigate this crazy world!"

I smiled in response and wondered why she was acting as if we were long-lost friends. I barely knew the woman and something about her just didn't sit right with me.

"Yeah, well," I smiled nervously. Something about Verena didn't sit well with me. She was overly eager to help me. What did she want from? Instead of pushing away the arm she tossed over my shoulder, I played it cool. "Hopefully, we will have time to make up for that one day."

"Absolutely!" she cheered and knocked her hip against mine.

In a moment of déjà vu, Verena was called away. Just as it happened outside the restaurant in New Orleans. And just as I did then, I searched for my exit strategy. Malachi tapped me on the shoulder, having returned from his conversation. An unfavorable expression on his face as he caught sight of Verena swimming away.

"What's wrong?" I asked as he placed his hand on my back, ushering me forward.

"Nothing, just catching up with an old friend." He shook his head slightly then frowned. "I just got an odd feeling."

"Do you need to go lay down?" I worried about him. Not twenty-four hours prior, he was a demon dwelling in the darkness. Malachi put on a brave face for me, but I wished that he wouldn't do that. How was I supposed to help if he kept his guard up?

"No, I'm fine." He forced a smile.

"Okay, so tell me about this journey I'm supposed to be going on. What do I have to do besides climb a mountain which is really a damn volcano and pluck this stone from its mouth?" As if that wasn't enough to ask of me.

"They call it the Naiad's walk," he started.

"Naiads, as in the nymphs? I thought they only lived in fresh water." I remembered reading about the creatures in the textbooks that Malachi gave me when he locked me in my room, away from all humanity. "What are they doing in the ocean?"

People also referred to them to as the river gods. I remembered staring at an image of one lounging on the side of a river and imagining being able to swap my life with her. The sun illuminated her skin, and she looked so free. I was sure her life was nothing of the nightmare that mine had become.

"True, but the particular nymphs earned a curse of their own for crimes committed against the covens. It is their duty now to protect the stones and to make your journey to retrieve yours, the most difficult possible."

"I see." My stomach knotted. "So, they won't be the gentle creatures I read about?"

Of course not!

"Well, every species has its bad seeds, you know. Don't worry too much about it. Like I said, you will have a guide that will go with you."

"Yeah, a guide that isn't you. What's the catch with this guide? You also said that they can only go so far."

"I told you I can't go. Whomever they choose will be worthy, and they will help you navigate the passages. They will only be able to go as far as they successfully reached on their own journey."

"Meaning that a siren who already failed is supposed to help me succeed?" I scoffed. The blind leading the blind.

"Yes, few have succeeded, and if you succeed, you can never return to Mt. Ononolo. If that were allowed, well, each successful siren would simply return with another, and all power would be restored. Not really a great formula for a curse."

"Who's going to be my guide?" I sighed and scanned the crowd. Every woman there wanted me dead. They'd all likely lead me right into a trap to end my life.

"Apparently, I will." Verena moved forward. The look on her face was no longer bubbly, friendly, or inviting. If I had to guess, I would say that at that moment, the girl wanted nothing more than to punch me in the face for simply existing.

"You?" My eyes darted between her and Malachi who offered only a shrug of his shoulders.

Big help he was!

"Yes. I tried, and I failed. Hell, I made it a lot further than anyone thought I would, so I guess I am as good of a guide as any." She crossed her arms and rolled her eyes. So much for forming a new friendship.

"So, you've been there. How does it really work?" I asked with excitement, but Verna avoided the question by waving to a passing man.

"Well, as you read, there are five challenges that represent the five families who broke the treaty." Malachi answered for her, drawing my attention briefly away from the upset woman. "They will test you in compassion, strength, bravery, greed, and lust. These challenges will form in different ways. Each challenge will present differently for you than they did for any other siren. Its unique to who you are. You must overcome them. Verena's job is to help you work through the challenges."

"Which one did you fail at?" I turned to Verena.

"The fifth." She looked past me into the depths of the ocean as if she were looking into a different time. "When do we leave?"

"I thought there would be some grand announcement." I shrugged. "At least that's what the books say. When a siren goes off to take her test, the people celebrate her courage. Right?"

"Yeah, well, apparently Chaney and the other uppity-assed mama sirens decided to forgo that for now. They thought it would cause too much of a stir. Most people here don't want you to be here and they damn sure don't want you coming into more power." She looked over her shoulder, distracted by something unknown. "Look, I'll meet you back here tomorrow morning and we can head out then. Does that work for you?"

"Um, yeah. Sure." I nodded because what else was I going to do? It wasn't as if I could tell her to give me a week so I could frolic in the sea without a care.

CHAPTER 3

***M**y task was to sit* in a room and wait for someone to come get me. Shortly after Verena left us, Chaney pulled me away from my protector. It seemed she was the only other person who was okay with having any direct contact with me. Even with her willingness, I could tell that there were other things she'd rather be doing than helping me.

Half the time I felt like she was being punished by having to operate as my handler. There were moments, however, when she would let it slip that I intrigued her. Sometimes I would catch her staring at me as if I were something she could dissect.

Before leaving me alone, Chaney offered some additional information about the tests I would face.

JESSICA CAGE

"Have patience, with yourself and your guide." She spoke as she checked my room. Again, there were people who didn't want me there. Had to be safe and make sure no one tried to sabotage me. "It's hard going back there, after failing. They're thinking about helping the next siren but reliving a terrible loss. You need to be open to the lessons being taught through your journey as well. And remember that you are strong, with or without your stone."

"Thank you." I nodded as she headed for the door.

"Do me a favor," Chaney wagged her finger in my face. "No sneaking off to your boyfriend's room tonight. We don't need you all riled up before your journey. You need a clear head."

"Can I just-,"

"No, you can't just anything. Stay in your room. Its one night. There will be plenty of time for you to spend with him after you return. Is that clear?"

"Yes," I nodded. "I'll stay in my room."

"Good, I'll have them send food soon. Going to need your strength." The burly woman left, cursing as her tail caught in the door.

I held in my laugh until I was sure she couldn't hear me.

As hungry as I was, I didn't want another underwater meal. Don't get me wrong, I loved fish. It's at the top of my go-to meal list, just as long as they cook it first. None of that raw stuff for me. But that was basically the only option. What I really wanted was a thick, juicy burger. There were no charbroiled burgers and crunchy fries under the sea. Now, that would be a great last meal!

I considered breaking Chaney's rule to visit Malachi one last time, but decided it was best not to.

He did, however, send me a message delivered by a reluctant friend. The nervous man with a full afro and an innocent smile knocked on the door and handed me the simple note.

"You got this. I believe in you, now believe in yourself. -M"

I read the note about a hundred times before I put it away. Each time, the tension in my gut worsened with the realization that I may never see him again. In her passive lessons, Chaney told me that not every siren made it back from the Naiad's Walk. The older woman was sympathetic enough to stay with me throughout my first night in Xylon and answer as many questions as she could.

Chaney was one of the sirens who tried to gain her stone and failed. Her trial ended at the third test. When I asked her what the challenge presented to her, she shut down, so I changed the topic. It was understandable that she didn't want to dig deeper into her failure.

Instead, we talked about life in Deuterio and about her family. She had two daughters, two sons, and a husband who was always away for work. She didn't divulge what work he did to keep him away, but she was all too eager to talk about how they frequently used the Mate's Doorway. When my face blushed, she knew I had a previous encounter with the lovers' portals.

The Mate's Doorway allowed a siren to be with her mate, even if they were on the other side of the world. Its magical properties created a private space where a couple could be with each other. Sirens needed their strength. What keeps a siren stronger than any other form of sustenance? Sex.

The doorways were all made from the sacred oak trees, which were rare and found in only a handful of places across the world. They harvested the seeds the trees grew from beneath the waters of Deuterio and planted them only in areas where the soil was rich and flush with magic. I learned that most of the trees successfully rooted in Africa.

After the war with the witches, the sirens planted the doorways across the world. Because they had to change the way they navigated the Earth, couples would often get separated. This way, they could still be together and avoid a siren going on the rampage because she was forced to go without.

While she recounted her own story, my mind went back to the doorway in New Orleans. The memory of my first encounter with the magical structure brought a somber air to the room as I pictured Demetrius's face. I touched my hand to my chest as I drifted away into a brief memory of an illusion of physical pleasure.

I didn't know what the doorway did, but it called to me. It pulled me in and with me came Demetrius. He touched, kissed, and tasted me in the empty space, and I enjoyed it. And then my heart ached because we lost him and I would never again experience that feeling with him. My cheeks flushed with red, and my gut filled with the twisting sensation of guilt. How could I be fantasizing about Demetrius while Malachi was suffering?

I slept very little that night. Each time I closed my eyes, the dark umber skinned, blue-tailed Merman with locs that fell near his waistline waited for me. He reminded me that there was so much about myself, and about the world that my unusual situation thrusted me into, that I didn't understand.

Breakfast was an assortment of weird underwater fruits, with flavors that were pleasantly unexpected. I devoured them, hoping a full belly would make up for the lack of proper rest and wondered why I hadn't had them sooner. A girl could only take so many fish platters.

Chaney arrived shortly after the food. She helped me by styling my hair, by pulling it away from my face into a long braid that fell down my back. She complimented me repeatedly, which gave me pause. Why was she so friendly now? Perhaps she wanted to lift my spirits before sending me to my death. How sick was that?

Verena was waiting for us, as she said she would be. Chaney led me safely to the meeting point, handed me off, and quickly swam away without even so much as a wave goodbye. That woman had some serious personality issues to contend with.

It was so early that the streets were empty. The only other person I saw was an old man who watched as Verena and I progressed through the city toward the dark waters outside of its boundaries. The strongest of siren magic enforced the boundaries of Xylon, like the other cities. It kept their people safe by preventing the creatures that lurked outside from getting in.

Some beasts that inhabited the waters of Deuterio were familiar to the human realm, like sharks and whales, but some were not. There was a time when a siren could roam freely. Each possessing their own power, they need not worry about what prowled in the depths. Defending themselves was never a problem. Times were different now, and without their own power to aid them, they were vulnerable. This effectively lowered them on the food chain. Just another delectable item on a menu for monsters.

"Where are we going?" I questioned my guide as we moved further from the limits of the city's light. The boundary was now behind us, and my anxiety was already on a rise. I wasn't ready to battle any beasts.

"The gates," she said, already annoyed with me.

My first choice for a conversation starter had clearly been the wrong one. I rolled my eyes at the back of her head. Sure, she could be justified in her frustrations. But I wasn't the one who asked her to come on this journey. How dare I have the nerve to show my ignorance of a world I'd never experienced before?

"The gates?" I tried to recall any information I had read or been told that would explain this unknown location, but I came up empty. Once again, this was something that someone deemed an unimportant detail until, of course, it wasn't.

"Yes, it's the access point where we will cross over. There is no other entrance to the path of the Naiads. You should know now that crossing through these gates will mess with your mind. Sometimes it will feel as though you are on land, but you won't be. That is where most people get lost.

"It will feel like you have already won, that you have accomplished what you've gone there to do. That is when most of the sirens who come here turn back, expecting to go home a champion, but once they leave, they realize their mistake and there are no second chances.

"You can't go back and try again. Once you fail, your stone, and the power it contains, is lost to you forever. The best piece of advice I can give you is to always remain focused on your goal and remind yourself of exactly why you are doing this. We all come for our own reasons, our own purposes." Verena wiped at her cheek.

Assuming she was removing tears, I placed my hand on her shoulder to stop her. "Are you okay?" I asked, and she turned to me. Her eyes looked as though she had been crying, but the thick darkness of the water made it impossible to be sure. Her voice held no evidence of her being upset.

"I'm fine. We need to keep moving." She pulled away from me and continued.

"What's the rush?" I was in no hurry to enter the land of mind trippy mess.

"Believe it or not, I have other things I need to do with my time besides babysitting you through this process." She snapped. "I would like to get this over with."

With that, it seemed we had nipped our potential friendship in the bud. Something always felt wrong to me about Verena, but now, as the bronze skinned woman continued her swim away from me, I knew without a doubt that she was hiding something.

Great, I had to go on what they had described as the most arduous journey of my life, and I had to do it with a woman I honestly didn't trust. Not that there were any other more pleasing options, but I'd be surprised if she didn't turn out to be the reason I failed. The sensation of a dagger being plunged deep into my back was unshakable.

I tried to stay as close to her as possible while we swam through the dark waters. My head filled with the warnings received from both Chaney and Malachi of the dangers that lurked in the open seas. Creatures like nothing found in the human realm, and yet the same dangers were there. Every now and then, my eyes would pick up of movement in the distance, as if something were teasing my peripherals and challenging my resolve. My ears would pick up a low tremor, and my flesh would feel a change in the vibrations of the water. Something was nearby.

"Do you feel that?" I asked Verena as I tried my best to scan the shadowed water but could pick up nothing but dark silhouettes of odd shapes that seemed more illusion than anything palpable.

"Feel what?" She continued forward, unfazed by my question.

Perhaps it was my nerves, paranoia, and uneasiness that created the imaginary dangers. I nearly convinced myself that my mind was working against me when I felt the disturbance again.

"That." I grabbed her hand, stopping her from swimming further ahead of me. "You can't tell me you don't feel that in the water. It's like something is pressing against me. I can feel it in my tail."

"Maybe you're just nervous because you're swimming to your death." She mused in poor taste, and had I not been nearing complete terror, I would have told her to work on the timing of her dark jokes. "Come on, we need to keep going."

"Verena, something is out there." The firm press of an underwater current convinced me that what I was experiencing was no simple trick of the mind.

"There is nothing. You just need to chill." Again, with the annoyed brush-off of my concerns, Verena refused to listen to me. She resumed her swim, and I followed as closely as I could.

The waters were calm for a few minutes, but then I felt it again. That added vibration to water, but it was more intense this time. There was more force behind the pressure and just as it ended, a low moan echoed it. Something was coming.

"Look, I know I am new to this world, but something isn't right here. Stop and listen, please!" I swam ahead of her, placed my hands on her shoulders, and forced her to pay attention to me.

"Fine! What exactly is it that you want me to do?" She huffed.

"Listen, just hear what is out there." I pleaded.

Verena closed her eyes, appearing to listen to the surrounding waters. She shook her head before opening her eyes again.

"Nothing, okay, I hear nothing. Now can we go?" She pushed my hands away from her shoulders. "Never do that again," she warned me, and for a moment, I could see something more behind her eyes. A budding hatred for me.

What could I have possibly done to her in the two times we met to make her hate me? We barely knew each other, and it wasn't as if it was by my personal request that they made her my guide. She had other things she wanted to spend her time on. Hell, so did I! I didn't ask for any of it.

"How can you not?" The moan was louder this time, and by the quick change in expression on Verena's face, I could tell that the sound of danger had finally registered with her.

"We have to get out of here!" She grabbed my hand, ignored her newly invoked no touching policy, and swam as hard as she could. Her tail pushed the water behind her in ripples that tripped me up for a moment, but soon I was in stride with her.

The noise grew in sound and intensity, and I pushed as hard as I could, but my body quickly became fatigued. Unlike the rest of the siren world, I was unaccustomed to the prolonged swimming. With the lack of sleep, my energy reserves were quickly depleting.

I kept up with her but wondered how long it would be before my tail would give out and Verena would leave me behind. This woman was not the type to sacrifice herself, especially for someone she so clearly despised. Just as the worry that she would abandon me crept into my mind, I saw a small shimmer of light in the distance, a beacon of hope.

"There! We just have to make it to that light. Come on!" Verena yelled.

The light was my focal point. It served as a line of hope. The closer I got to it, the more likely my survival. When my body felt as though it would crash, my mind screamed that we were almost to freedom. Just as I thought we would make it, that ray of hope turned to dark despair as an enormous mass of a beast moved between it and us.

With the reflexes of a cat, Verena changed her course. She swam upwards toward the surface. I followed her, but my tail felt heavier with each passing moment. The distance between us spread further, and my heart sunk to the pit of my stomach. Was this the end for me?

I scanned the waters as I pushed towards the top and could finally see what was after us. The higher we swam, the more I realized just how massive our predator was. Its dark flesh blocked out everything beneath us, and it stretched out in every direction for at least a mile.

Verena pushed harder, and I found the strength to do the same. Finally, we broke the surface of the water. Barely taking a breath, she pushed on and swam along the brink of the ocean. I followed her, but I could hear the thing coming. In my peripheral, I saw its scaled back appear above the edge of the water. It was close.

"Watch out!" my warning cry to Verena came moments too late.

Verena's body disappeared beneath the water, snatched by the beast. She struggled against its attack, but she wasn't winning the fight. My chest burned as panic filled me. What was I supposed to do? I swam toward her. If I could free her, we could still make it.

The light of the sun filled the sky above, making it easier to see her. I stuck my head beneath the water and nearly choked at the sight. The massive beast in the water beneath us had eight tentacles that stretched in all directions, with one wrapped around my guide.

I swam quickly, trying to avoid contact with the thing. I expected it to grab me with one of the other seven appendages, and frequently dodged attacks that hadn't come because its focus was Verena. Like it had a vendetta. It shook her body around like a toy. Her arms flailed and she screamed for help.

"I'm coming!" I called to her, but Verena had already lost consciousness by the time I reached her.

The large tentacle that was wrapped around her waist constricted her body, limiting her ability to breathe. I grabbed her hands and pulled as hard as possible, but she didn't budge. My grasp on her remained firm. To let go would be to lose her because the monster descended and was hauling Verena right along with it. I couldn't allow her to be taken by that thing. I needed her.

"No!" I yelled at the beast. "You can't have her!"

Instinct took over, and I whipped my tail out, smacking it into the appendage that held Verena. It took just about all the energy left in my body, but it was well worth it. The heat of electricity bolted through me and in a stroke of power, it ripped out of the tip of my tail.

The ocean air quickly washed away the smell of searing flesh. The monster cried out, its howl muffled beneath the water, and its tentacles slammed against the surface and caused large and forceful waves. I kept my hold on Verena, who was finally free of our attacker's death clutch. But we were still in imminent danger of being knocked to the ocean floor.

I threw her arm over my shoulder, grabbed her by the waist, and swam as hard as I could. The added currents produced by the monster's tantrum threw off my sense of direction. I could only hope that I was moving in the gate's direction and not putting us further from safety.

"Okay, Verena, it would be really helpful if you woke up now!" I grunted as I carried the dead weight of my unconscious guide.

The surrounding waves were only becoming stronger, and they pushed against my body and made it even harder to carry my load. She finally came out of her state of unconsciousness just as the loud smack of tentacles hit the water and caused a ringing in my ear. The beast was trying to kill us. Another boom of water being disrupted, and Verena was almost caught again.

"Swim!" I yelled at her, and she kicked into motion. Just as we broke free of the tangles of water and scaled flesh, I looked back to see two massive eyes, both green with strikes of red, staring at me. I could swear the thing winked at me, as if to say it would wait for my return.

"There, it's just over there," Verena spoke before diving beneath the surface of the water to our beacon.

CHAPTER 4

*W*arm air, *the smell of grass* and wildflowers wrapped around me, producing a staggering sense of calm. I breathed it all in and sighed. My toes clutched green blades as I walked across the field. The sun felt amazing on my skin, and I opened my arms to welcome it and to soak up as much of it as I could.

Body completely bare, the sun's rays warmed the skin of my chest, and any sense of shyness I once had left. It felt too good to be concerned about anything as frivolous as societal protocols for layers of man-made fabric. Thoughts of liberation, peace, and love looped through my mind. This was what I'd always wanted, freedom.

In the distance was a line of trees that waved to me as their limbs moved in the breeze. Standing near the foot of the tallest tree in the center of the grove was the figure of a man. The silhouette was tall and had broad shoulders. Something powerful drew me to him.

In three steps, what looked to be at least fifty yards became a few feet. With the lessened distance between us, I could see him. Locs fell past his shoulders as he stood there, body as bare to me as my own to him. He smiled and my heart lurched as if it would escape the confines of my chest.

"Syrinada." Hearing my name coated in his deep tone, I smiled widely and took the last steps to place my body against his. Waiting arms wrapped strength and security around me, and I lifted my arms to drape around his neck as I nuzzled his shoulder with my nose.

"I can't believe you're here." I held on to him tightly and refused to let go for fear that he may no longer exist.

"Where else would I be?" His hands fell to my waist, but I still held on.

"I thought..." What did I think? I couldn't remember, but I knew the man my arms clung to so forcefully shouldn't be there. It was an instinctual feeling that was difficult to ignore.

"What did you think, Sy?" His voice was different as he whispered in my ear.

It held the same deep timbre as before, but with something more. The sound, the undertone of a metallic growl, was sinister. I slowly released my hold, dropped my hands, and stepped back from him.

"You're not supposed to be here, are you?" I shook my head. "This isn't right."

With a quick step forward, he pulled me back into his hold, his touch adding to my confusion. This time it was he who clung to me. I pressed my hands against his chest, urging him to give me space. I needed to think, to clear my head, but his strength overpowered my own and kept me there.

His lips began a trail just beneath my ear, which moved down my neck and finally landed on my collarbone as my head fell back with a nervous sigh. Memories of the one time I'd experienced such intimacy with him returned, and I struggled to maintain my poise. Keeping myself together became even more difficult as his hands massaged the flesh of my back and gripped my ass.

"And where should I be if not here with you right now?" His voice vibrated the flesh beneath his lips and my pulse quickened.

"You," words were fleeting, as my mind tried to process the feeling of his touch versus the thoughts I wanted to verbalize.

"I," he moved his tongue in light flutters across my skin and leaned deeper into me.

"Demetrius." To say his name brought a clarity that had been unachievable.

I shook my head to remove the cobwebs of visual deception, and the short action gave me a quick glimpse of what was true. For a moment, perception clashed with reality, and beauty became ugly and desolate. The entire scene, the trees, lush grass, and wildflowers highlighted by a bright sun amongst a clear sky, it all turned and revealed the charred ruins of a land that once was.

It wasn't just the scenery that changed. He changed and could see him for what he truly was. This wasn't my lost friend, the brother of my protector; it was a monster. It was something evil wearing the mask of someone I held close to my heart.

"You're not supposed to be here. I remember now. We had to leave you because they hurt you." Anger gave me the ability to push away from him. I stumbled back and nearly tripped over a fallen branch.

"Sy," He reached for me again, but I dodged his extended hand. Something in my gut screamed for me to get away from him.

"How could I do this?" I backed away further, guilt creeping up. "How could I fantasize about you like this with everything that's at stake right now?"

"It's not a fantasy." He tried his best to convince me of the lie. "I'm here with you. Be with me, Syrinada."

"Then what else could it be because I saw you die!" I screamed. The sound of my voice echoed back to me and caused the surrounding realm to once again flicker to a more disturbing version of itself.

"Sy." His hands never stopped reaching for me, but I refused to let him touch me again. If he touched me, I might forget what he really was.

"Stop saying my name. This isn't right. Malachi, he is hurting right now. He's back home mourning the loss of you, his brother. Here I am betraying him. I'm supposed to be focused." I searched the area but kept sight of him as well. Where was Verena? Why was she not there?

"Focused on what?" He reached for me again and again.

"On getting my stone. I need it. I have to protect myself, to protect him and everyone else who is now in danger because of me."

"So that's all you're here for, for power?" He growled a bit with the question, and it stopped my search for my guide.

"I couldn't care any less about having power. I care about life and about my life and my friends. It's up to me to protect them. How can I allow them to hurt because of me? You lost your life because of me! I can't let that happen anymore." I yelled at him. If he were who he truly claimed to be, he would have known that.

"Sy, please calm down, baby. Just come back to me." It was the voice of a monster attempting the cooed his pleas for my return to his arms.

"I said stop calling me that." I cried.

He stepped toward me again. When I refused his touch again, he roared. A lion on his deathbed. With his teeth bared, long strings of saliva dripped from his mouth. He cried out again, and the lush green scenery behind him dissolved into the ash of a forgotten land.

The man in front of me transformed into a shadow of his former self. Flesh melted from his face briefly to reveal the contoured jawbone of his demon side before his form liquefied completely and left in front of me the emptiness of the forsaken grounds.

The surface beneath my feet turned hot, and I looked down to not find the grass that I gripped between my toes, but stones, which cut into the bottom of my feet. Harsh winds that slammed against my naked form in icy blows replaced the warmth of the sun and light as a dark cloud rolled in. I clung to myself, not sure what else to do.

I jumped when the heavy cloak fell across my shoulders to block my flesh from the wind. I eagerly grabbed hold of it while searching for the person responsible for placing it there. Relief washed over me as I found my guide standing behind me.

"We have to move." Verena's voice was a welcomed tone, which soothed the edging of fear in my mind.

"We crossed the gate?" My teeth chattered; how could it possibly get so cold so fast?

"Yes, and now we must find shelter before the storm comes in." She responded with an unexpected stiffness to her tone.

"Are you mad at me?" I pulled the cloak closed and allowed the hood to fall over my face for more protection from the unwelcoming environment.

"No, let's go." She lied, but I chose not to call her out on it. Now was not the time.

"There's a storm coming." She looked to the sky, and I saw what reflected in her eyes as I followed her view. Massive clouds of black with branches of lightening that struck the ground beneath them were quickly rolling in our direction. Fires flared where the bolts touched before the rain drowned them. "If we get caught in that we won't be making it much further."

"Where are we supposed to go?" I could see nothing but emptiness around us. All signs of vegetation were wiped away with the illusion of Demetrius. "There is nothing out here."

"There!" She pointed off in the distance, where if I squinted hard enough and tilted my head, I could see what appeared to be a small elevation. "There will be caverns we can hide in."

"And if there aren't?" I questioned.

"Then you better hope like hell that storm breaks before it reaches us. Now come on." Verena took off running.

I pulled the cloak tighter around my naked form as the wind picked up and the mist of water from the storm we were trying to outrun reached us. The water had an odd smell to it. It wasn't the calming scent that usually came with rain, no matter how torrential the storm was. This smell made me nauseous, and I had to swallow back the bile that threatened the back of my throat.

Verena held her own cloak close to her body as we ran, and she gagged from the revolting scent as well. The sound of stone shifting beneath my feet, and the feeling of the sharp edges cutting into my flesh, were painful reminders of all that I would have to go through.

That was only the beginning. I thought of Malachi because my mind would go nowhere else. He was my place of comfort, the one part of my current life that brought me peace. I thought of his touch, and I could feel the places on my skin warm in an echo of the memories, as if he were there with me.

"Snap out of it!" Verena screamed just as lightning struck the ground nearby.

A wall of fire shot up behind us. The blast was so strong it knocked me off my feet.

CHAPTER 5

I slid across the ground. Sharp-edged rocks cut the palms of my hands as I tried to brace myself. Tears flooded my eyes, but instinct told me to keep moving. Despite the pain, I made it back to my feet and scanned the area to find Verena. She kept running but looked back at me.

"Come on, get up." She called out. "We're almost there."

With the sound of another lightning bolt hitting the ground, I started running again. My body screamed from the pain in my feet, legs, and hands, but I had to keep going. I couldn't fail, not before I completed the first test.

"What the hell was that thing back there in the water?" I asked Verena as we made headway. I could better see the mountain and it looked to be the haven we hoped for.

"Kraken," she offered a simple reply as thunder cracked overhead and we increased our speed.

"You mean that thing is real, the Kraken, as in *Pirates of the Caribbean*?" I referenced the movie, which had been a favorite of mine. The scene when they called the Kraken to take out the ship was one I watched about a hundred times. After finding out that the thing was real, I had to reconsider my appreciation for the creature.

"Yes, the Kraken, as in Greek mythology, is a real thing," she said with attitude. "Do we have to have this conversation right now?"

"The distraction of conversation makes running for my life a bit more bearable." We continued to run and were making headway. "I can't believe the Kraken is a real thing."

"Well, if sirens, demons and witches are real, why not the Kraken?" She grunted, jumping over a large rock that I nearly fell over.

"Shit... I guess you're right."

"Look, there are a lot of things in this world that you are going to be exposed to. Things you would have never believed in your wildest dreams could be true, but they are. The best thing you can do is exactly what I did." She paused focusing on her run.

"And that is?"

"Besides, not holding lengthy conversations while running for my life?" She huffed as we continued running. " Syrinada, you need to accept right now that absolutely everything you can think of and even things you can't are indeed possible. Trust me, it will make life much easier."

Finally, we reached the foot of the small mountain and started our climb to safety. Blood dripped from my palms as I gripped the rocks to pull myself up. Luckily it was a quick climb to the cliff where a spacious cave set. Just as we made it inside the first shelter that we could find, the storm reached us. The cavern was adequate to keep us safe from the downpour, and lightning-caused fires.

The opening of the cave allowed for a perfect view of the devastation caused by the storm. The terrifying scene also brought a conflicting therapeutic feeling that rolled over me. Each time the lightning struck the ground, the lands would erupt in an array of orange and red blazes.

It targeted what little vegetation that existed, annihilating all signs of life. The rain that carried the putrid smell extinguished the fire but left the earth a blackened echo of what it once was. I thought there was nothing left, but when I looked closer through the downpour and the smoke, I saw it.

In the middle of all the destruction, there was still life surviving the storm. Small blades of green were barely there but held on to life. Witnessing that small show of strength gave me hope.

"How long do you think this storm will last?" I asked Verena without turning from the view.

"Who knows? It could be a few hours or a few days."

"Days? What are we supposed to do in here? What about food? How will we survive?" That took my attention from the storm.

"Okay, don't get yourself worked up when we don't know what's going to happen. Neither of us can tell the future, so there is no sense in trying." She'd been scouting the cave, but there wasn't very much to it.

It was standard for what I expected of a cave. Three sides that worked as walls, a curved ceiling, and that was all. It held nothing that could sustain us, and there were no connecting branches to escape to.

"I don't want to fail at this, Verena," I admitted honestly.

"Yeah, no one does. It won't help to put any unnecessary pressure on yourself. As if there isn't already enough of that to go around. You need to relax."

"Fine. I'll relax." I adjusted the cloak on my shoulders. "Tell me about yourself, Verena."

I figured, if we were going to be stuck in the cave, we might as well attempt to get to know each other better. It didn't look like our time together would be short-lived.

"Hmm... what do you want to know?" She laid out her cloak on the floor at the furthest point from the entrance and sat down.

"Why did you try to get your stone? I know everyone has their reasons and they aren't always as simple as wanting power." I sat next to her, but kept my cloak wrapped around my body. She laid out in the nude. I couldn't bring myself to do the same.

"Straight to the heavy hitters, I see," she laughed. "Well, my reason was simple enough. I wanted to prove my mother wrong. She never thought I was good enough to survive this world. I guess she was right."

"No, she wasn't, you're still here. I mean, most women who try this fail, right? That is the way it's designed." I stared at the ceiling. "You're no worse off than any of them. Take into consideration that you made it further in your test than most do, and you're actually doing better."

"Yeah, well, a lot of good it did. I haven't seen my mother since the day I returned, empty-handed and powerless." Verena shrugged, as if it meant nothing to her. I could tell she was only trying to mask the truth.

"I'm so sorry, Verena," I paused. "What about your childhood? What about before the test?"

"I grew up in the south, hence my accent. My family traveled a lot and all the while, I thought it was because of my daddy's work. I would of course find out later that the reason we had to keep uprooting our lives was because my mother had a hard time keeping her hands out of the cookie jar, so to speak. A year or two is all we would ever have before she would slip up and suck some local man dry and we would have to move."

"Did your mom get her stone?" I perked up. If her mother could suck a man dry, she must have had her full power. "How were you able to be on land?"

"Like most people of our kind, my parents found a loophole in the rules. There were witches out there who disagreed with what happened to our people. An entire race punished for the acts of a few. They reached out and offered their aid. Charms and spells allowed safe passage for those who accepted their help." Verena shifted, uncomfortably recounting her past.

"And no, my mother didn't have her stone. Contrary to popular belief, there are some sirens who can still take the energy of a man with or without the stone and we still have some pull over humans. It's all the other awesome stuff that comes along with it we lose.

"Anyway, when given the option to leave her home, my mother jumped on it. She hates the sea. She prefers two legs to one tail, no matter the power in it. I'll never understand her preference. When I finally found out what we were, I begged her to take me to see our home.

"One day I found an old chest. It was one of those things she would usually keep tucked away out of sight. It had notes, drawings, charms, and so many artifacts I would have never believed were real if I hadn't held them in my own two hands. Hell, if not for the pictures of her with her tail, I would have assumed my mother just had a weird obsession.

"Anyway, my mother refused to take me. For three years, we fought about it before I turned eighteen and left on my own. It didn't take long to find others. I stayed close to the areas I read about in those papers. Eventually I found someone to show me all that I needed to know, a guide of sorts. He was a godsend."

"What do you do now. Now that you've finished your quest, and you know what you know about this world. What comes after all of this?" It was something that really worried me. Was I expected to just go on like none of those amazing and unbelievable things had ever happened to me?

"To be honest, I still haven't figured that part out. It's not as if I'm doing much with my time now. I enjoy life and use what limited powers I have to get the things that I want and need. It's not like anyone has come banging on my door with a list of demands. Well, besides helping you on your journey now."

Her answer was so passive. I'd imagined Verena to be doing much more and achieving greatness, but it appeared she was just floating through her life. What was stopping her? She didn't seem like the sort to just allow life to happen to her.

"What about the things you want for yourself? What about your goals and ambitions?" My curiosity increased.

"Ugh, and now you're sounding like my mentor." She rolled her eyes. "When I got back, he was on top of me about making a plan for myself."

"Sorry." She was right; I needed to chill out before she shut down again.

"No, it's fine. It's one of those things that has been coming to mind a lot lately. A girl can only skate so far through life." She rolled to her side, her back to me. "I'll figure it out."

The conversation died after that. Verena asked not one question about me, despite having said she wanted us to be friends. Eventually, we both decided that sleep was necessary. We laid together for warmth, using my cloak as a blanket, and attempted to rest.

Neither of us successfully accomplished a restful slumber. My mind ran in circles considering all that I would have to face and by the tossing and turning Verena did, I could tell the state of her future heavily weighed on her mind.

I woke up when the sounds of thunder and lightning stopped, and when I looked at the opening to the cavern, my jaw dropped. Standing in front of us, blocking any hope of freedom, was a wall of water. While we rested, the water rose, but somehow it didn't flood the cave and drown us in our sleep. I stood from the floor and walked over to the doorway to get a closer look.

I reached out to it and found the water cool to the touch. I expected it to fall in on me and crush my body beneath the weight, a punishment for disrupting its tranquility. Instead, it held. Ripples that were stimulated by my fingertips shimmered along the surface before it stilled again.

Verena pushed by me. "Let's go," she ordered as she stepped across the barrier and instantly left legs for tail.

The woman had no fear, no hesitation, and once again, no patience. While I stood there watching in awe, she started swimming away. I took a deep breath, not for air, but for nerve and stepped out. My foot never touched ground.

My tail emerged and pushed my body forward. We swam in silence upwards because there was no other way to go. A tunnel of smooth stone that slanted towards the sky had replaced the open field we ran through.

Rays of sun shimmered at the top, and I hoped the light was a good sign.

CHAPTER 6

*E**choes of laughter that mixed*** with cries of anger and despair, bounced around us. The further we swam, the louder the cries, until finally the weight of the water we left behind us muffled the unsettling noise.

After a brief silence, we broke through the surface of the water and sounds of the forest rang out around me. Birds chirping and scuffling sounds of animals running across the forest floor were welcoming. The deep current of the river pushed against me and I looked down to see my tail still attached, but the depths of the ocean gone, becoming just another figment of my imagination. I swam in a slow circle looked for my guide. Verena wasn't with me. There was no sign of her on the ground or in the river.

"Syrinada." The voice that spoke my name was a trill of a sound. I turned my head in the direction it came from but saw nothing.

"Yes, who's there?" I called out but wasn't sure what to expect in return. For a long while, there were only more of the sounds of the forest.

"Syrinada." There it was again, but once again, the source was invisible to me.

"Please, show yourself," I pleaded. I was eager to see what creature could produce such a sound.

"You must pass the tests. There are five." It spoke words that were full of meaning, yet I found it difficult to get past the sheer joy the sound brought to me.

"Yes, I know, but please." I wanted to see her face. I imagined the voice belonging to a female. One that would be more beautiful than anyone I'd ever seen before.

"Benevolence. You must have compassion for others. Believing you are any better than those around you, or that your needs are greater than the common good, is a sure sign of a corrupted soul. A siren must take care of her people."

"Please," I swam in circles, but the voice only continued its speech.

"Spirit. A coward has no business wielding such power. It would equal total devastation. Your spirit tells all about your ability to face arduous tasks.

"Perseverance. Proving yourself will be no easy one to achieve. You will suffer, but you must rise above. If you cannot, you will fail.

"Voracity. With power, will come the possibility of obtaining almost anything you want. It would be so easy to use that power to bend the wills of others and take that which does not belong to you.

"Lust. The desire for men and their energy earned your people this punishment. If you cannot withstand the urge to feed from them, you will never get your stone. We will not unleash your kind to bring destruction to humanity as you once did before."

Finally, she appeared to me. Golden hair that shimmered with light tints of pale green fell past her shoulders and into the water to drift out around her body. Bronze toned flesh glowed with the warmth of the sun. Large emeralds peered brightly at me from behind long lashes. A thin pout set above a rounded chin curved just slightly to hint at a smile. She stared at me.

"What is your name?" I asked in a nervous breath.

"My name is unimportant. It is not your goal to know my name," she said simply, and the start of the smile vanished.

"What is my goal? I know I am here to get my stone." The desire to be closer to her was strong, but I fought against it. She didn't seem like the sort to want to be okay with her personal space being invaded.

"Your goal is no stone." She responded firmly. "Your goal is to prove yourself worthy of the possession of the power the stone represents. The stone itself is but a mere symbol."

"What do I have to do? I'm ready and I will pass these tests." I tried to put on my best bravado. If I could appear in any way more ready than I was, maybe it would please her and she would give me more help.

"How can you be so sure of yourself when countless others have fallen before you?" She shook her head in angry disapproval. "The ego of a siren, just like all of those before you!"

"I didn't mean to offend you." I shied away. Her angelic appearance no longer appealed to me as she displayed her anger. It felt like a trap. I'd already fallen for one beautiful deception and was not looking to sign up for another.

"Offend me? Your entire existence *offends* me. If you didn't exist, I wouldn't be made to stand here, trapped for all eternity, and forced to protect something so sacred, which I am not allowed to obtain no matter the test I conquer!" she yelled but did not budge. My instincts told me to run, but in my heart, I knew that was the wrong thing to do.

"It doesn't really look that bad here." Point out the bright side that would surely work. She dwelled in a pseudo paradise. She had a conquering jungle, bright skies, a life of abundance. What could she possibly have to be so miserable about?

"You think that is because you see it with the eyes of a child!" The smooth sound of the nymph changed into a dark shrill as she spoke.

Her voice reverberated around her, and as if it were a tool she wielded with her hands, it ripped away yet another illusion, a deception to my eyes. The world fell silent, and the calm breeze became stale air. All sounds of life fell to an eerie echo of nothingness. This enchanting nymph frowned and morphed before my eyes. To watch it was slow and agonizing, as if I was experiencing her pain.

Bronzed skin became a pale blue. A side effect from years of being trapped in the dark and given only the artificial light provided by the imaginations of hopeful sirens. Her flesh was dry and raw thanks to the salt in the water. Her people belonged to fresh springs and rivers. The salty seas did nothing but damage to her natural beauty.

If I were to touch her, that skin would easily peel away beneath my hands. The golden waves of hair were heavy, and dark, weighed down by the salt of the sea. That glint in her eye had become a somber glaze animating the intense sadness and unhappiness she had suffered.

"If it weren't for your kind, there would be no need for my people to be here!" She cried and tears fell down her cheeks. As I thought, pieces of her skin fell away with each tear that slid down her face. The salt of her own tears scrubbed away the worn flesh of her face.

"This was a punishment for you as well as us." I spoke before giving thought to what words flowed from my mouth. "You're not here just because of what the sirens did. You committed your own crimes. Unlike the sirens, they didn't punish all the naiads, just those of you who sinned."

Yes, everything I said was true. It was what I had read while waiting alone in my room in Xylon, and it was what Chaney told me before I left. The naiads were just as guilty. Some of them were brutal and unkind. They were greedy and murderous. Just as the covens protected the humans from our kind, they did the same with the naiads. Only some would consider their ruling much more favorable for the river nymphs.

This woman, as beautiful as she first appeared, was here because she did horrible things.

"You know nothing!" She screamed, and the guilt of her past was clear. My accusation struck a nerve.

Something inside me urged for me to apologize but it was too late for that. She lifted her hand to the sky and with an angry cry smacked the surface of the water, creating a current so strong it sent me flying from the river.

CHAPTER 7

The feeling of being catapulted through the air was both terrifying and exhilarating. The nameless nymph was done with me after I went off at the mouth. I should have expected the response. What person wants to be called out about their dark past by a total stranger? One who came to them in need of help. The thrill of my involuntary exit from the water ended when my ass smacked the forest ground.

When I looked back to the flowing water, I saw no signs of her, but the beautiful facade of the forest was back in place. Now on two legs and fully clothed, I stood up and cringed at the pain left behind from the impact. Verena sat nearby on a fallen tree trunk eating a handful of strange colored berries.

She just smiled, but I could tell she wanted to laugh. "So what is it?"

"What's what?" I grunted from the pain.

"Your clue, she gave you a clue, a riddle, or something that you would need to decipher." She paired the continued chomping of fruit with a look of expectancy. "What was it?"

"She didn't give me a riddle." I dusted the dirt from my ass. "She just turned ugly and gray before she snapped and kicked my ass to the curb... literally."

Verena rolled her eyes with a heavy sigh. "What did you say?" There I was again, adding to her frustration.

"What do you mean?" I played dumb. I knew my slip of the tongue caused the impromptu ending to my meet and greet with the river nymph.

"You had to have said or done something wrong for her to react the way she did." Verena stopped snacking and gave me a look that threatened physical violence.

"Okay, I said something. I didn't think it was that big of a deal, though. And everything I said was true." As if that made it any better.

"Oh, god, what did you say, Syrinada?" She shook her head.

"I told her it wasn't just the sins of the sirens that landed her here," I blurted out because it was obvious her response would be one of disapproval.

Verena laughed. "Are you being serious right now?" She stood from the makeshift bench.

"What?" I eyed the berries she tossed between her hands and hoped she would offer some to me.

"Nothing. I mean, I'm in awe of your genius. Piss off the one person who could offer any tool to help you." She shook her head and looked at the sky. "What a great plan."

"How was I supposed to know that? You didn't tell me that would happen." I retorted.

"Excuse me. I thought the need to be nice to the nymphs was an obvious thing." She spread her arms and spun in a circle. "They control all of this. You know that. Why should I need to explain that to you? It's called common sense!"

"Okay, so I didn't get a clue. I can still figure this out." She was right. I didn't think before acting and because of that, I was left grasping at straws.

"Right." She laughed mockingly. "Good luck with that."

"Look, this has to work, okay? I can't go back without even having done the first test."

"Did she say anything significant to you of significance?" Verena titled her head scrutinizing me.

"Let's see. She told me the five things that they would test me on. Compassion, spirit, perseverance, voracity, and lust. That much I already knew before coming here, thanks to Chaney and Malachi." I tried to recall as much as I could of the brief conversation. "She also called me childish, though I would have to disagree with her."

"Anything that might actually help us out here?" Verena crossed her arms over her chest and tapped her foot on the ground.

She was over being stuck as my guide. How could I blame her? Here I was, a siren with limited knowledge of things she considered basic information. It didn't matter to her that it wasn't my fault I knew nothing of this world. She had not one ounce of concern over whether anyone had taught me the fundamentals of being a siren. After hearing her story, how could I really complain? She started off with just about as much understanding as I did, and somehow, she came through it all.

"Well," pacing the ground, it seemed like the talk with the nymph was so long ago. The memory of her voice was already fading from my mind. How was that possible? I fought against the forced lapse in my mental capacity and tried my best to remember what had just occurred. "She questioned me about why I was here. It's hard to remember, like something is trying to steal the information from me."

"Well, you better fight to hold on to it." Verena pointed at me and shook her head. "Your memory is all that we have!"

"I'm trying!" I walked faster, the increased speed somehow helping to jog my memory. "She said I have to prove myself worthy of the stone."

"Care to expand on that a bit? As nice as it is that you can remember something, it doesn't exactly help us out right now."

"The stone is just a symbol and not the goal." I stopped and stared at Verena, who rolled her eyes. "Look, I'm not being cryptic. Those were her exact words."

"That makes no sense. The stone is the goal. I mean, yeah, proving that you won't be susceptible to the things that caused the stripping of our powers in the first place is key. But all that is more of a mind game, a test of will. The physical stone isn't just some symbol. When claimed, we literally absorbed the damn thing into our body. Why would she say that about you?" A gaze sharp enough to cut flesh was an accusation. Verena either suspected me of withholding information, or she was about to go on a serious and unnecessary rampage.

"Do you think that was the clue?" Finally, there was something to be hopeful about, one thing that I didn't screw up, and possibly enough to stop the death stares Verena kept shooting my way.

"I'm not sure. It could be, though it would have been nice to hear everything she had to say. I guess complaining about that would be the same as crying about spilled milk. Won't change a damn thing." Verena tried to rain on my singular parade, but I had to hold on to the hope that I'd done right.

What else did I have to get me through the ordeal? Something told met in the days to follow I would need every bit of motivation I could get. My faithful guide would not give me that.

"If you think about it, it actually makes sense. It fits into the norm, or the not so norm of my life." I reasoned. "Everything else about my mythological existence has differed from what everyone tells me it should be, so why not this?"

"That's it." Verena's eyes lit up like a kid piecing together their first puzzle. "You're different. Everything about you beginning with your conception has gone against the grain."

"Yeah... I know." It was all anyone could say to me. My entire life was different and messed up. It wasn't exactly something that was easy to forget.

"No, I mean, think about it. You already have your own power, Syrinada. Think of how you handled that Kraken back there." She pointed backward as if the thing would rise from the river. "There is no way I would have been able to defend us. If it weren't for your power, we would have died. Your father was a witch, which meant he had powers, right? His powers were ones he was born with. He didn't have to earn them. Maybe that magical element in your genetic makeup is active. If that is the case, you aren't just trying to gain your siren power. Reaching your stone would unleash a new power entirely."

"So, you think she meant I need to prove that I am worthy of that new power?" I dropped my head to look at the passing clouds. This just kept getting better.

Verena, so delighted with her logical puzzle solving, paid no attention to my pending breakdown. I would have been just as happy, but the idea of earning even more power when I could barely control the abilities I had scared the hell out of me.

"Apparently." She shrugged, as if it had all suddenly become so simple.

As if it wasn't two seconds ago, she looked like she would do cartwheels around the damn forest. To Verena, we were now on a cakewalk, but in my mind, things had just gotten a hell of a lot more complicated.

"Great. So what do we do now?" I asked.

There was no way in hell I would let her know how my own dread was choking me. My mind scrambled to remember the function of breathing while she enjoyed her momentary triumph. It wouldn't matter either way. Even if I fell over and peed my pants from the fear of what was to come, I still had to face the music. There was no turning back and no easy way out.

"Now we keep moving and find somewhere where we can rest. Something tells me that this place won't be so pleasant once the sun goes down." As if on cue, like a well-plotted movie, the aggressive grunting of what I pictured to be a very large and furious bear sounded off in the distance.

In everything I've ever seen whether it be a nature show on cable television or in a blockbuster movie, whenever anyone ever found themselves lost in the wilderness, they looked for water. Every single time the goal was to find a body of water and stick close to it.

Having recalled this bit of handy information, I suggested that we stick close to the river. Not only was it a natural resource we would need for our survival, but it felt safe there, comforting to know that it was nearby. My guide, however, overruled me and said that we should move on.

I questioned her about reasoning for this total and complete denial of my foolish idea.

"No challenge or test, whether in this realm or back in the human one, ever happened in places of comfort." She reported as if she'd rehearsed the line a thousand times before.

To succeed, we had to step outside the box. It would have been wonderful to disagree with her. It would have been fulfilling to laugh in her face and tell her how completely moronic she sounded. Unfortunately, I wouldn't be doing either. Verena was right.

The entire point of the Naiad's Walk was to challenge myself, and to prove myself capable of being greater than I was. Lounging by the riverbed, though highly enjoyable, wouldn't exactly be a great way to accomplish that.

"You know, I'm actually enjoying this place this time around." Verena's back was to me, but I could hear the smile in her voice.

We walked away from the safety of the flowing waters. The forest felt more alive the deeper we moved. Though likely all a part of the illusion crafted by the gamekeepers, the place was buzzing with wildlife, and it worked to put me at ease.

It would have been much worse to move through the tall trees and push past the low-hanging branches if there had been nothing but eerie silence. It was exactly what I expected, that every test, every single part of the challenge, would be weighed down with silence. I expected to feel like I'd been deserted. Instead of a blank slate of torture, there was life, warm and welcoming, despite the occasional sound of distant howling.

"I just bet you are. You weren't the one being hurled through the air like a rag doll." I dusted my pants off once more and frowned. Whatever my ass had planted so firmly into was not coming off. My stomach growled as I watched her pop a small reddish berry into her mouth. "What is that?"

"A snack," with that, and as if she didn't realize that I was starving, she popped the last few into her mouth. I'm not sure why I had any expectation of her offering some to me.

"At least we have clothes on this time around." I turned my attention to the appreciation for the jeans that covered my legs and the boots that protected my feet from the harsh surface of the jungle floor.

"What? Don't tell me you're against showing off a little flesh." Her laughter echoed through the trees and frightened a group of birds, who quickly took flight.

"Not exactly, but I highly doubt it would be favorable to be naked in a place like this. Just think of how vulnerable that would make a girl." I pointed to the cluster of spiders that hung from the tree limbs just ahead of us.

"Oh, hell no!" Verena jumped back and quickly changed her path.

The way she shimmied as if the eight-legged pests had taken up home beneath the layers of her clothing caused me to burst out in laughter. I doubled over, clutching my sides as she dusted her hair and checked for webs.

"All right, you've had your laugh." Verena straightened, her face as red as the berries she refused to share with me. "Now, let's get a move on. We don't want to be out here all day."

"Which way?" I stopped as our alternative path brought us to a fork.

There were two distinct passages, one that lead to an open field to our left, and to our right was another that wound deeper into the jungle. My gut told me the easy terrain of the field was not the way to go. It would leave us out in the open and should we run into one of the howling beasts, there would be nowhere to hide.

"We need to find higher ground. It would be great if we could secure another cave." Verena scanned the area. "The problem is, I doubt we'll find one out here that isn't home to some predator. I'm not trying to be on anyone's meal plan."

"Alright, caves are off the house hunting list." I nodded and followed her lead as we headed to the right and deeper into the jungle.

CHAPTER 8

*S**weat poured down my brow** and stung my eyes. I blinked to ease the pain. My heart raced and my lungs strained to keep up the demand for oxygen. It took all my strength to keep pushing. The muscles in my thighs and calves burned and suffered from continued spasms.

It didn't matter the pain. I had to run; I had to keep moving. Each time I thought I'd give out, the roar of the beasts that chased us boomed in my ear and provide all the motivation needed to force me to continue.

Five of them, black panthers, each the size of bears were hunting us down. We'd stumbled across their sleeping den. Usually panthers are solitary creatures. They liked to be on their own, but these were clearly no ordinary cats. We'd tried to make it out before they sensed our presence but were unsuccessful.

I can't say how long we'd been running, or how many trees we slipped through to avoid close calls as we reached a cliff that sent two bi-pedaled sirens and five burley felines tumbling down a steep slope.

At the river, we lost them. Funny how that worked out. The place of safety, where the silly and naïve newbie siren wanted to stay, was where we once again found security. As much as I wanted to brag, I thought it best to keep my mouth shut and not rub Verena's nose in it. Besides, I was too preoccupied with running for my life to stop and gloat.

We jumped into the river and swam with the current. The beasts didn't cross into the water as if frightened by it. Though I figured big cats like them wouldn't have such a fear, but trust me, I wasn't knocking anything that helped save my ass. Instead, they ran along the opposite side of the river and kept their eyes on us. In an odd turn of fortune, the river ended in a waterfall.

It dumped our lovely little siren tails into an enormous pool of water about a hundred feet below. The fall left me disoriented, but I cleared my head and swam to the surface. I searched the waters and found relief when Verena popped up a few feet away from me. She pointed to the top of the waterfall where our predators were. Looking up, we could see them as they watched us and calculated the best path down.

"They'll find a way down here. We need to keep moving." Verena pulled my arm as she swam towards the far end of the water, away from the waterfall. "I think I'm bleeding. I hit something hard when we landed. We have to get out of this water. I don't want to find out what the hell is living in here."

"Yes, okay." We swam to the edge, climbed out, and ran into the tree line.

Once there, Verena checked her body for cuts. She had some bruising on her left and side, but she wasn't bleeding. A good thing too, because blood would make it easier for those beasts to track us down.

I had a few injuries myself, but nothing that would make us more vulnerable to the predators hunting us. As it stood, we could only hope that the wash of the water would make it hard for the burley felines to catch our scent again. Motivated by the frustrated roar of the panthers who struggled to get down from the cliff, we got up and started running.

A few minutes into our sprint to safety, something caught my attention. My legs skid to a halt as my brain connected with the information my eyes had collected. To the right of us was an area that looked severely overgrown, which was hard to say, considering where we were. Barely visible beneath bushes filled with red vines that looked sharp enough to cut bone, was a bloody hand.

"What the hell are you doing? Let's go!" It pissed Verena off that she had to double back to find her student who was not on her tail as she thought but crouching beside what looked to be a poisonous bush.

"Wait, someone is over there." I looked around for something that I could use to move the vines and give us a better view.

A fallen branch became the tool of choice. I struggled to push the veins away but succeeded. The parted bushes revealed the body of a woman. She was young, and her body was so frail, it looked like she hadn't eaten in weeks, maybe longer. Her skin was pale and dried blood covered most of her body. Closer examination revealed multiple wounds that were already caked at the openings with a mixture of blood and dirt.

Her wounds weren't healing and as I got closer, I had to hold my breath because of the stench of decay that came from them. I didn't want to imagine what type of beast could have brutalized her body in such a way. If I did, I would have to consider the fact that the same monster could still be nearby.

The girl was severely hurt, but the slow rise and fall of her chest and the slight flutter of her eyelids when she heard my voice told me she was a fighter who had yet to give up.

"We have to help her." I looked back at Verena, who looked at me like I'd lost what little sense I had.

"How exactly do you expect us to do that?" Verena kept a close watch on our surroundings. So far, there was no sign of the panthers, but we both knew that it didn't mean we were safe. Clearly there were other hazards to worry about.

"You want to just leave her here to die?" I looked at her in complete disbelief.

"Look, we'll cover her up. Hide her, and after we know it's safe, we can come back for her." Verena gave me the band-aid response. Just something to shut me up and get me moving again. She knew damn well that if we left the girl, there would be no going back for her.

"You want to leave her here covered in all of this blood? You know those things will find her and you know that there is no way we're going to come back here to make sure she survives this." My disbelief was hushed but direct.

"Right. She is covered in blood! They will use that scent trail to lead them right to us!" she scoffed. "But sure, you're right. I hadn't thought of that!"

"We won't leave her here like this." I stood firm in my decision.

It wasn't right to walk away. Verena was my guide, but it was my journey, my test, and I had to do whatever felt right in my gut. Leaving that girl there to suffer and die alone and in agony was not the right thing to do.

"Fine, it's your failure, not mine." Verena threw her hands up in the air, completely fed up with me. "If we're going to do this, we better hurry!"

After a quick search, we chose a hollowed tree trunk as our mode of transportation for the unconscious girl. With some deliberate effort, it became a makeshift gurney. We used thick vines as straps to secure her battered body into the hollowed half. The entire time we worked, Verena's attitude worsened and with every disgusted glance she threw my way, my mood darkened.

I couldn't believe the level of selfishness. How dare I want to save a life! Shame on me for not wanting to leave this woman there to be a victim to even more torture! Those panthers might not have ever found her had we not come running her way. It was because of our presence that she was now in even more danger.

I couldn't think of what they would do to her. I felt the need to help her. It's what I would want someone to do for me. It was what I wanted someone to do when I was being kidnapped by a psychotic, drugged-out rapist. No one was there for me; I would be there for her.

"We have to stop her bleeding and cover up her wounds. It looks and smells like they're already infected." Verena worked to further secure the straps, unaware of the mental tongue lashing I was giving her. "Hell, at this point I'd be surprised if anything out here would even consider having her for a meal. That smell is just..." She stopped, as if contemplating something, but left the thought unspoken. She shrugged it off and continued working.

"What could have done this to her?" I looked around. "Do you think it was another panther?"

"From the look of her wounds, it was an animal, but no panther did this. Look at the openings in her arms and torso. These are slash marks, they look like something a knife would do only more rigid, and they're all singular. A panther has claws, close together. They create a pattern which isn't here. I would say another human did it, but look at the bite marks on her arms. It looks like she was defending herself from something." Verena paused again with an unsettling look. "This mark here, on her shoulder, it's like a symbol. I know it somehow. Something about this feels familiar, but I can't place it."

"Well, hopefully whatever it is, is long gone or has at least found something else to focus on. I don't want to see the thing responsible for this."

"She's secure." She stood after securing the last strap. "We need to move. I don't feel safe here."

Verena scouted the area with her eyes and relaxed her shoulders after she found nothing to be concerned about. We weren't in immediate danger, but she was right. We were vulnerable out in the open. If the panthers didn't get us, something else would be eager to take their place.

We carried the woman between us and alternated between who took the lead. Verena, of course, reminded me at every opportunity of how much time we were losing by hauling her with us. We made frequent stops so we could rest our arms and each rest stop put us further behind the sun. We needed to find shelter before nightfall.

Just as we made it to higher ground, where we felt safer, we heard the roars of the panthers. They were still looking for us, and they were close by.

CHAPTER 9

*V*erena proved to be more of an outdoors woman than I would have ever expected. Quickly she created shelter, building a tepee from a collection of sticks and plants. It was just enough to give us cover, but not enough to make us stand out in the night.

Revealing her caring side, she made a salve for the girl's wounds. She used two oddly shaped rocks as a makeshift mortar and pestle. In it, she created a medicine from a variety of plants, sap, and honey. We worked to create bandages from large leaves and cleaned her wounds with water collected from a nearby stream that seemed out of place, but I chose not to question it.

We also fashioned two makeshift canteens and filled them with water for drinking. By the time we finished our tasks, the sun barely kissed the edge of the sky. The coming blanket of darkness made my stomach turn.

"What are we going to do? We can't just leave her here." I swallowed a mouthful of water and bit into the wild fruit that Verena deemed safe to eat after we watched what looked like a cross between a skunk and a rabbit run away with an armful. If the wildlife would eat it, it would be safe for us... or so we hoped.

"Look, we don't know anything about this girl. She could be the enemy." Verena sat on the other side of the fire we'd made, warming her hands. Eventually we would have to put it out, the light would attract predators and we were not prepared for a fight. "What if they sent here her as a distraction, something to slow us down?"

"Why do you jump right to that conclusion?" I put my water down. The topic was already moot and to bring it up again only brought more unnecessary frustration.

"Why don't you?" She sighed. "Why don't you question the validity of the things happening around you? You just automatically accept everything at face value. You need to be more critical thinking."

I shook my head and tossed the partially eaten fruit aside. It left a weird taste in my mouth, anyway. "Excuse me for not automatically assuming the worst in a person. After all that I have been through, I'm surprised myself that I can still see the potential good in someone. I try not to make a habit out of judging people before I know anything about them. This girl hasn't said or done anything but lay there and suffer and you've got her branded as an enemy."

"Look, I don't know what you think this is, but let me tell you, you're wrong. Be worried about preserving your own ass right now, not the ass of some half dead woman you don't even know. It's not just your life on the line right now, okay!" Verena looked away from me.

For the first time, I realized she was afraid. So was I, but that fear didn't mean that it was okay to abandon our basic sense of decency towards another living soul.

"I really wish I could understand how you can be so selfish." I stood up, ready to walk away, but I stopped. She wouldn't win this; I wouldn't just let her say whatever she wanted to me without voicing how I felt. "On second thought, no I don't."

"Oh, spare me. You want to call me selfish, yet throughout your entire life you have left a trail of devastation behind you. Clearly you don't care how the hell it affects anyone else." She stood as well, putting us back on even ground.

"Excuse me?" I whipped my head around to look at her, offended by her candid opinion.

She had made such a ridiculous generalization of everything I'd gone through, and then placed the blame on me. My life was no cakewalk, that was damn sure, but it was not a life I had chosen. No one considered my opinion when they plotted out my existence.

"Of course you don't see it. You're so self-involved that you don't even realize what you're doing to everyone around you."

"You are completely delusional. You have no idea what you're talking about!" I was losing control of my temper. How could she think it would be okay to say any of those things to me?

"Really? Your entire existence has been nothing but a pain in the ass for everyone who comes anywhere near you!" She was yelling, disregarding the fact that we were in a jungle and there were predators all around us.

"Since when are you such an expert on my entire existence? You don't even know me." Despite her sudden disregard for our safety, I tried to keep my voice at a leveled tone. "The only reason you are here is because they forced you to be."

"Oh, I know plenty. Hell, everyone does! Both of your parents' lives were ruined because of you. Your aunt had to vacate her home to protect you, and the Denalis; there are countless losses in that family because of their efforts to keep you hidden; including Demetrius!" Her voice broke when she said his name and she slammed her eyes shut and turned away from me. She knew him, but how?

"Just drop it, okay?" I frowned but didn't ask about her connection to Demetrius or why it seemed to hurt her to speak his name. Maybe she knew he died. Maybe she was a scorned lover. Either way, it didn't matter that she was hurting, not after everything she had just said to me.

Pinning the death of my parents on me, and the betrayal of my aunt, was unfair. She claimed to know so much about me but formed her opinion on speculation. Just like everyone else had.

"Or what?" She turned back to me with eyes red with anger as if ready to fight me. A bully prodding its vulnerable opponent.

She almost got what she wanted. She almost had me ready to let go of my common sense and fight her right there. Almost, but then I recognized the feeling that crept up from deep within. It was the same one I got before someone ended up in a human shaped pile of ash. I took a deep breath and focused on calming the building rage. Whatever happened, I couldn't let it come to that.

"Or nothing, just shut up. I don't have to listen to this." If I trusted her not to kill off our new travel companion I would have walked away but I couldn't do that. We had to stay together. The moment we made it back home, Verena could go to hell for all it mattered to me.

"Yeah, you do. What else are you going to do? Where are you going to go? Face it; we're stuck out here with each other. Now, because of your selfishness, we are going to be hunted down. We probably won't make it through the night with her here." Verena pointed to the body of the girl who still clung to life. "When we die, you make sure to thank your little pal over there!"

"Helping another person is hardly a qualifying trait of a selfish person." I rolled my eyes. "Besides, I'd think you would be happy if we failed. The faster you got to go home."

Fatigue was setting in and arguing wasn't helping anything. Verena obviously had her own issues with me, but that was her problem to deal with, not mine. Whatever feelings she had against me, she would have to put that shit to the side.

"Look, we're going to be fine. We'll take turns and sleep in shifts, which we would have had to do even if she wasn't here. I'll take the first shift." I offered a solution to what she thought was a problem.

The best thing to do was to approach this with a clear head. Consider all that we knew of our situation, and then make the best of what was available to us.

Verena wasn't happy that I hadn't fed more into the fight. It was like she was waiting for anything to give her a reason to claw my eyes out. There were more important issues at hand, such as surviving the night and making sure that the injured girl was safe.

We covered the girl in large leaves beneath a layer of dirt. It would keep her warm and hopefully mask the scent of her blood. Verena muttered again about this being a mistake before she finally went to sleep.

The sun disappeared during our argument, and darkness enveloped us. We put the fire out to make sure we remained hidden. I settled into my position and watched the last few embers as they died out. The sounds of the jungle resonated in the surrounding darkness.

Night critters skittered across surfaces. My mind played tricks on me. My skin crawled and the hairs on my arms stood as I imagined things crawling across my flesh. It became hard to distinguish between the sounds that I really heard and the ones my overactive imagination created.

The rustling of a snake moving across the ground nearby was real, but the indistinct sounds of deep growls that were barely there were not. I kept telling myself it was my imagination.

Deep, rhythmic breaths became necessary to center myself and refocus on the world around me.

The only comfort came from knowing that if danger were near, my heightened senses would warn me. As it was, I could hear everything from the critters to the birds overhead in their nests. I could see much better at night than I ever could before.

The nosy squirrel that was about ten yards away from us was as clear to me as if he was standing right next to me. He became a welcomed sight, as he would dart away only to return and stare at me longer. Once he came back with a snack. A small nut that he nibbled on while looking over at our campsite.

I lasted through my shift and was relieved that nothing out of the ordinary happened. It was Verena's turn, and she barely said two words after I woke her. She moved into position to take over the watch. I lay down to rest but fear overpowered exhaustion, making it difficult to fall asleep.

There was no telling what would be thrown at us next, and I hated to admit it, but having the unknown girl with us was just as dangerous as Verena said it was. Regardless, I wouldn't leave her behind, and I damn sure wouldn't allow Verena to toss her to the panthers to buy us more time.

CHAPTER 10

I woke up to what felt like the heat of a thousand suns prickling my flesh. I covered my face to block out the bright rays. Sweat drenched my skin and added an uncomfortable weight to my clothes. The braid Chaney put my hair in had come undone during the run and sweat and mud had the heavy strands matted to the back of my head.

I looked over to find Verena sleeping. Head leaned back against the tree, and she was snoring like a grizzly bear. She was so concerned for our safety and yet she slept through her watch! Lucky for us, we survived the night. I sat up, grabbed the makeshift canteen, and poured some of the remaining water into my mouth.

The thought passed through my mind to pour the water over my head. It would have been refreshing, but I didn't need another reason to be lectured by my spiteful guide. The unconscious girl came to mind. She would no doubt need hydration after the way we'd bundled her up. Hopefully, she would drink. We couldn't get much in her mouth the night before.

I got up and walked over to the small bedding we put together for her and panicked when I found it empty. The girl was gone. I searched the area for signs of a struggle, but there weren't any. It was as if she vanished.

If any of the beasts in the forest took her, they would have made noise and would have awakened the both of us. Hell, they would have attacked us all, not slip off with the only one that wasn't a fresh kill.

As Verena pointed out, that girl would have been the least appetizing of the three of us. So how in the hell was she missing? I turned to an exhausted-looking Verena. Of course, she looked like that. How else would she look after deliberately going behind my back and disposing of the "problem".

"What did you do with her?" I kicked Verena's leg to wake her.

"Excuse me? What the hell is wrong with you?" She sat up and swiped at my leg, but I moved back and avoided the hit.

"Don't play innocent, Verena. I know you got rid of her. How could you do that?" It was obvious what she did, and playing dumb wouldn't convince me she was innocent. Regardless of how she felt about me, this was my journey, my test, and she had no business interfering in that way.

"You have lost your mind." She yawned and stretched as she stood. "Don't kick me again."

"Have I? How else do you explain why she is suddenly missing?" I pointed to the empty place where we left the unconscious girl.

"Hell, I don't know. Maybe she got up and walked away." She grabbed the canteen and shot an aggravated glare at me as she wiped the sweat from her forehead.

"Right, the unconscious and injured girl just got up and walked away. Do you honestly expect me to believe that?" I crossed my arms over my chest and waited for whatever brilliant excuse she could concoct.

"I honestly don't care what you believe. I didn't touch that girl." She pulled her t-shirt over her head, leaving her in a thin tank top. "I don't owe you an explanation, and I am damn sure not about to stand here and be put on trial. I said I didn't do it!"

"We have to find her." Though I didn't want to believe her, I did.

The logical part of my brain finally pulled itself from the lingering slumber and highlighted the obvious details that I'd overlooked. Logically, the scene just didn't add up. We could barely manage lifting her together. There was no way an exhausted Verena could have disposed of her alone without a struggle and without waking me up.

"Why exactly do we have to find her?" She fanned herself and scanned the campsite frantically. I didn't know what she was looking for, but whatever it was didn't jump out at her.

"Because she could be..." I trailed off, unsure of my explanation.

I couldn't understand why I cared so much about the girl, but I did. She was hurt, and she needed us. She needed me. My heart felt heavy as I thought of the girl on her own, alone, and now probably being tortured even more than before.

"What? You think she could be hurt? The girl was already messed up when we found her. She could be dead. Yeah, to be honest, that is a possibility. I'd be surprised if it wasn't the same thing that attacked her that came back for her." Verena looked up at the sky. "How in the hell is it so hot out here? I mean, I feel like the sun is touching me! Back the hell off!" She yelled at the sky; the woman was losing her mind.

"Why would it just take her?" None of it made any sense; every new option seemed more ridiculous than the last. A predator only wanting one person when there was a feast of choices didn't seem very that likely to me.

"Maybe it only took her because it only wanted her. Have you ever thought of that?" When I didn't respond, she continued talking to offer further explanation of her theory. "Something that I learned when I was here was that a lot of these creatures out here, they mark their prey. It's not just about a meal, it's about the conquest. That girl was marked. By what, I do not know, but it claimed her. We should just thank our lucky stars that it didn't choose to take us!" Canteen in hand, Verena turned to head to the stream to collect more drinking water.

"Verena?" She had to be wrong about what she said. If not, we were screwed because what I saw when she turned her back to me was no birth mark.

"What is it now?" She dropped her head back but didn't turn to me.

"What is that on your shoulder?" I pointed at the mark that I knew hadn't been there before.

I'd spent most of our time together, staring at the girl's back whether we were swimming from a Kraken or running from panthers. Besides a small tattoo of a butterfly just above her waist, her skin was clear, flawless.

"What?" She tried looking over her shoulder to see what I was referring to, but couldn't.

"It looks like the mark that was on the girl." I stepped closer to evaluate the marking. "I think it's the same symbol."

"What the hell? Are you sure?" Her eyes were a mirror of complete terror and I could do nothing but nod. Whatever mutilated that girl put its mark on Verena. If what she said was true, it would come back for her.

"We need to get out of here before…" I didn't get to finish my statement because just then the sounds of howling echoed out around us.

"Shit!" Verena crouched down and scanned the surrounding trees.

"Maybe it's just the panthers?" I offered.

"Yeah, because that is just so much better. Five bear sized cats, would be a lot easier to deal with than one mystery creature returning to kill me." She whispered harshly. "We need to get our shit and get out of here!"

For once, we didn't debate our next move. Quickly, we gathered what we could and left our camp behind us. As we moved, I wondered about the girl. I hoped she was okay, but the sharp pain of intuition in my stomach when I thought of her told me she wasn't.

I'm not sure what I expected to happen. It wasn't as if I believed we stood a chance at saving her life. We wouldn't have been able to carry her far before the blood loss and infections took over. Regardless of knowing the truth of our situation, dying with us caring for her and providing whatever limited comfort we could, was better than being torn apart by whatever took her.

We were careful not to leave a discernable path for whatever beasts were trying to follow us. I could hear things moving around us, sounds that I hadn't noticed before in the elevated hills. My focus had been on the girl. For a moment, I considered that Verena might have been right. The girl was a distraction and a setback. If we'd left her there, perhaps the monster wouldn't have marked Verena, but still my resolve hadn't changed. We did the right thing in helping that girl.

"Here, we can set up here. We need to rest and I feel like complete shit right now." Verena dropped her makeshift bag to the ground.

When she turned to face me, I had to suppress my need to gasp at her appearance. Her skin looked odd, the coloring was different; she had become paler, even though the sun had been toasting our skin, and I was about two shades darker. Her eyes were jaundiced, and the yellow tint made her look sickly though just hours before she was in perfect health.

"Verena, are you okay? You don't look so good." The longer I examined her, the more sickly she appeared.

"I don't feel so good either, but that is beside the point. We need to set up shop, we need to make sure we can protect ourselves." She looked over my head at the large tree behind me. "Up there, it should support the both of us easily."

"You want us to set up in the trees?" Was she even capable of climbing that high? My worry shifted from the unknown girl to my guide. Would she survive another night?

"Yes, it's off the ground and hidden. If those panthers catch up with us, we stand a better chance of losing them up there." She didn't mention the other thing that we both knew was trailing us. It was better not to.

"Panthers can climb trees." I pointed out the flaw in her logic. Besides, there were plenty of good reasons for not sleeping in a tree. Reasons like falling to our death.

"True, but we will be ready if they try." She picked up a long stick from the ground and smiled.

CHAPTER II

*V**erena showed off her*** nature girl prowess again, but instead of creating salves and bandages, she went to work crafting weapons of defense. She painstakingly worked to sharpen rocks into points that were sharp enough to pierce our enemies' flesh. When satisfied, she tied the rocks to sticks using vines she had me pull from the trees and forest floor.

I paid attention to every detail and learned all that I could from her. Though my work was much slower, I still added to the heap. Before climbing the tree to rest, we did some target practice, and my accuracy surprised the both of us. She found us more fruit, which we rationed, and drank the last of our water. We would have to find more soon, or we wouldn't survive the heat of the jungle much longer.

The sound of talons scraping against wood woke me from an odd dream about cloud watching. I looked around to find the animal life in the trees that surrounded us, quickly evacuating their homes. Even in their hurried exit, they weren't the source of the sound that woke me.

Squirrels leaped from limb to limb in scattered patterns as they moved further and further away from us. Birds flew away in frenzied escape. I tapped Verena on the leg to gain her attention. She looked worse than when we laid to rest. Her complexion was now green and I would never tell her, but she smelled. It wasn't just the stench of a woman who hadn't bathed in about a week, but the smell of sickness, the smell of death.

"Wake up." I continued tapping her until her lids lifted and her eyes focused on me. "Something isn't right."

The sound rang out again. Nails grating against wood and stone.

"What is that?" she asked and sat up. She put her hand to her head and clung to the large branch she rested on.

"Are you alright?" She didn't look it.

"Yeah, I'm just tired." She reported, but her eyes were full of worry.

"I don't know what is making that sound, but whatever it is, it is freaking out the animals." I pointed to a neighboring tree where another flock of birds took to the sky. "Look, they're all leaving. I think we need to follow suit."

Verena nodded in agreement, but before we could move, the tree shook as something slammed into the trunk. If not for the tightened grips of the roped vines that secured us in place, we both would have fallen to the ground below.

Several of our makeshift spears shook from their ties and into the darkness below. My search to find them ended with the sight of something that would haunt my dreams for years to come. This thing was pulled straight from the depths of the darkest mind.

Six hairy legs stuck out from a large grey body the size of a small truck. Its face was a collection of eyes of various sizes, too many to count, all gray and yellow. On the ends of its legs were sharp singular talons, on its head a horn, and it had a tail; the tip of which was an exact match to the markings left on the girl we tried to save. I screamed the moment I saw it and turned to look at Verena, who was in a state of shock.

The damned thing was trying to climb the tree we were in. The second round of pounding against the tree snapped her into action. She cut the ropes that held us in place, jumped to a crouching stance, and told me to brace myself. A moment later the tree fell.

The moment it hit the ground, we jumped, grabbed any weapon we could, and ran away from our campsite. There was no time to second guess ourselves. The sound of the devastation the beast caused as it chased after us motivated us to keep moving. It demolished the jungle around us and small creatures that could not escape its path succumbed beneath its weight and the sharp claws that pierced the ground.

I was behind Verena, watching as she pounded against the ground and forged ahead. Watching her gave me hope we would survive. Even in her weakened state, body sick and putrid, she still fought to survive. At that moment, I was cast in a shadow as the monster leapt over me and crashed into my guide.

Their bodies tumbled as they rolled across the ground. Verena dodged every pass of the sharp hooks that was aimed at her. In a last act of desperation, she used her spear and punctured the belly of the beast. It cried out and fell away from her. That moment of relief was followed by another moment of terror as it wrapped its tail around her waist, rolled onto its side and they both disappeared.

A wave of water smacked me in the face and pushed me back onto my butt. When I sat up, I was at the edge of a large body of water that, a moment before, was more of the lush jungle spread around us. There was no sight of Verena or the monster that had tackled her.

Disoriented by the sudden change of environment, I tried to focus on the issue at hand. Verena was in trouble. The only thing I could assume was that the beast had pulled her under. I had to go in after them. I had to help her. My stomach turned as I considered all my options. I couldn't leave her behind.

Without further thought, I jumped into the water with the last spear in my hand. My tail quickly formed and aided my dive. A trail of bubbles I saw ahead of me was my only lead to their probable location. I hoped they wouldn't dissipate before I found her.

An aggressively enticing odor flooded my senses, a mixture of blood and fear. The amount of blood in the water meant Verena's injuries were bad. I pushed harder quickening my efforts until Verena came into view. She was trapped, her tail pinned beneath a rock, making it impossible for her to escape on her own.

Surveying the area was pointless. The deeper I swam, the darker the water became. I could only see so far, which gave the beast plenty of space to hide. It was completely silent. Even my advanced underwater hearing didn't help.

It was obviously a setup. Verena was nothing more than bait. The creature was a smart hunter. As Verena said, it enjoyed the acquisition more than the kill. It understood me. Verena needed my help, and there was no way I would leave her there to become monster chow.

"Go!" The weak sound of her voice broke the silence just before I made it to her. Blood spilled from her lips. Even under the water, she looked sickly, like she would give out at any moment.

"Not without you." The odds of saving her looked no better after I reached her, but that wouldn't stop me from trying.

"It will kill us both. There is no way you are going to get this thing off me by yourself." A futile push on the boulder was all she seemed capable of.

"Look, I'm not leaving you here to die, okay? I know you're weak right now, but I really need for you to help me, please." I pushed the boulder that pinned her tail with all my strength.

Verena tried to help, but with the large gash on her left arm, the more she pushed, the more blood spilled from the laceration.

"Fuck! This isn't working." The frustration was nearly crippling, but it wasn't enough to make me quit. It just meant that the obstacle needed to be reevaluated. Sheer physical strength wouldn't get the job done.

"I know, just go." She looked at me. "I won't blame you, you have so much you need to do, you need to finish your test and get your stone."

"No. Wait. I have an idea." I swam back a few feet and hoped like hell that I could reproduce the same power that freed us from the Kraken. "Cover your eyes."

When she did, I whipped my tail at the boulder. My first attempt barely did anything. The second hit was stronger. The boulder rocked and a few small pieces of it broke off and fell to the ocean floor. It wasn't much, but I knew I could do better.

The third time, I cleared everything from my mind before trying again. With the impact it split nearly in two. I gave it one more focused hit and with that, Verena was free. There wasn't any time to waste. As soon as she was free, that thing would come. The chase was on.

As gently as possible, I pulled her healthy arm around my shoulder and swam towards safety. My tail felt weak and Verena felt heavier than the first time I had to carry her weight, but I pushed as hard as I could to get us out of there.

"It's coming," Verena said, and I heard the beast as it wailed behind us.

I swam harder, though I knew I wouldn't be able to outrun it for very long. I had just enough strength left in me. If I could strike it as I did the Kraken, hopefully that would do the trick. I had to wait until it was close enough. To waste the shot would mean losing the little advantage we had.

The movement of the water gave up its location. The closer it got, the more turbulent the currents became. Its efforts to catch us produced an underwater tide that threatened to push us off course.

Catching one of its hairy legs in my peripheral, I stopped swimming. With my free hand, I threw the spear I'd kept with me out into the darkness. It cut through the water and pierced the flesh of the beast. It didn't stop the thing, but judging by its cry of pain, my effort wasn't completely wasted.

"I have to go back." The thought made my stomach hurt but I couldn't deny what had to be done.

"What?" Verena asked. "We need to get out of here."

"It's injured now. I need to take advantage of this opportunity. Its only going to keep coming for us unless we end this now?"

"Are you sure?" She asked, worry in her voice. "You don't have to prove anything here."

"Yes. Do you think you can keep going without my help?"

"Yeah, I should be okay." Verena nodded and I let her go.

I watched her progress to make sure she was okay before I swam in the opposite direction back into the depths of the dark waters.

It wasn't long before I found it. The cluster of angry eyes locked onto me before its enormous mouth spread open to reveal rows of jagged teeth that could easily tear me apart. This was my chance, and it was the only one I would get.

The surge of power moved within me. Hot like fire and stronger than I'd expected, it pooled from the pit of my stomach and traveled down the length of my tail. I stopped my swim and aimed the tip of my tail directly at the open chest of the beast. The explosion of light and heat created a force that blew Verena and me towards the surface and the beast straight to the ocean floor.

I watched in disbelief as the life drained from its falling body. With its teeth still bared, it turned into stone and disappeared behind the dark wall of the water.

Verena finished the swim to the surface with minimal help. I thought I could recreate her salve to put on her wounds, but when we made it out of the water, we were no longer in the jungle. Instead, we sat on the sandy shore of a white beach. I found relief to be away from the harsh terrains, and the creatures that lurked around every corner, but disappointment sunk my stomach. Along with its dangers, we also lost the healing herbs we needed.

I helped her to the tree line of what I assumed was a small island and was grateful for the makeshift knapsack that, despite the hectic start to our day, remained strapped to my shoulders. There wasn't much left to our load, and what we had was damp from the water, but luckily, most of it proved to still be viable.

I immediately went to work on Verena's injuries, patching what I could, and placing cool compresses over her swollen shoulder. She barely said a word, just stared at me, and whenever necessary, corrected my actions. Once I constructed our camp, I sat and watched over her.

The island was silent, eerie in its emptiness. I wanted to explore and see what was out there, but I couldn't leave Verena injured and unconscious. Instead, I watched as the sun fell from the sky and the bright blue waters turned into a blanket of black and reflected the stars from the sky.

It happened then, as I struggled to keep my heavy lids from falling. A shimmer of gold reflected off the sur water. I stood and walked to the edge of the sand and turned to find its source. Behind us stood a massive mountain that wasn't there before. I'd been staring at the skyline above the trees for the entire day and not once had I noticed its presence.

It shimmered in the night as if sprinkled with gold dust, creating a breath-taking image. The movement of lights performed an enchanting dance that lulled me into a trance. An invisible string connected to my core pulled me forward towards the glistening elevation.

My head filled with dreams everything that I could do with all that gold. Life would be so much easier, and it wouldn't even be necessary to go back home, where my life would once again be in danger. I could buy my own island and hide away forever with Malachi by my side. He would gladly accompany me. Neither of us would have to hide who or what we were. We could heal from our wounds in peace.

My legs carried me forward, driven by both my longing to be free of the chaotic mess my life had become and the spell that had enraptured my mind. Sounds of the waves, which once crashed loudly in my ears, became distant echoes. They were merely lapping sounds that tickled the back of my mind and attempted to remind me of something important, but nothing felt more important than this.

Trees faded away as I neared them. Each one vanished and cleared a path that made my goal easier to reach. My lazy smile stretched further across my face as my feet met the base of the mountain.

This was no mountain, not in the standard definition of the term. The formation that protruded from the earth's surface was a massive collection of dust. Golden flakes piled as high as my eyes could see. The breeze would pick the flakes up and move them away, but each time they would recoil and rejoin the mound.

I watched the magical dance and swayed with delight. I picked up a handful and let the flakes slip through my fingers. The cool touch elated me and the dream of my island with Malachi became the hope to secure the island that I stood on for myself.

Small steps, which belonged to something I could imagine being no bigger than a mouse, approached me from behind. Instinctually, I put my back to my newfound treasure, and prepared to defend it against anyone or anything that dared to come near it. It was mine now. I found it. The call of the cool dust was a magical feeling, and no one would take it away from me.

CHAPTER 12

*F*or *hours, I alternated between various stages* of in-sanity. One moment I would be dancing giddily through the gold, tossing it in the air and letting it rain over my skin before it left me and returned to its place. The touch of it was sensational. Then a strange sound would alert me to an unseen threat and I would turn feral. By the time the sun returned to the sky, my eyes were bloodshot and my body ached from exhaustion, but I was happy. I had my mountain all to myself.

"Syrinada?" My name rolled off the enemy's tongue.

The voice and face were familiar, but it didn't matter to me. She could only be there for one reason, to take my found treasure away from me.

"What are you doing?" She asked approaching me with slow steps.

"Get back!" I yelled at the sickly looking girl and picked up the spear I had crafted after the third interruption of my golden dance.

"What the hell is wrong with you?" She stepped back, and I zeroed in on her injury.

There was no way she could overpower me. She clutched her left arm to her body. It was an obvious point of weakness that I would use against her if she made any attempt at taking my gold.

"It's mine. Not yours. You can't have it!" I yelled. "Leave my island. Leave me alone!"

"Okay, clearly you've lost your mind. We don't have time for this now. We have to figure out what's next." She coughed and put her hand to her chest.

"Leave!" I screeched and launched myself forward. I slammed my hands into her chest and she stumbled back landing against a tree.

"You want me to leave? Fine! I don't need this. You will be the one trapped in this ridiculous wonderland for the rest of your life, not me!" She held her arm tight to her side as she limped away and mumbled under her breath. I grinned; victorious because I had secured my riches.

"What are you doing?" The quizzical voice was deep, melodic, and the words came as lengthy strings of singsong.

I turned around to find a tall man with gray hair and a large, toothy smile. His ashen skin hung loosely from his bones. Yellow eyes stared out at me with greedy delight. He wanted my gold. He could never have it!

"Protecting what is mine!" I yelled my feral proclamation.

"Oh, silly girl, none of this belongs to you." He laughed and stepped forward just enough to elicit a hiss from me. "This is not yours. This is mine."

"No, it's not. I found it. It is mine." Again, the sick sound slid across my lips, which only evoked a deeper laugh from the strange man.

"So just because you stumble across something, that means it belongs to you? Where do you get such convoluted logic?" He took a step forward and held his hand out to the mountain of golden dust, then waved at it. The shimmering mound shifted as the dust twirled and moved at his command.

"Stop it!" Panicked, I yelled at him and tried to grab the golden flakes he'd stolen. Each time I'd thought my hand had captured them; I'd open my fingers to find my palm empty.

"If you want it, you may have it." He snapped his fingers, and the dust came together and fell to the ground in a solid brick. My eyes widened with joy. I could finally hold my treasure.

"I do!" My wide eyes echoed the greed of this magic man. I reached down for the gold but he wagged his finger in my face.

"There is just one condition." He sang with a smile.

"Anything." I fell to my knees grabbing the gold and held on to it as if it were my lifeline.

"You must make a choice. The girl or the gold." The tall man stepped aside and behind him was the same sickly girl, the familiar enemy. Spellbound by his wicked magic, she held a knife to her own throat. "Payment must be made; one small sacrifice and you may have all that your heart desires." He grinned and tilted his head to the side as he waited for my decision.

As I looked at this girl with her terrified eyes, and her hand that held a knife to her own throat, I actually considered allowing her to use the blade to open her veins and relinquish her of her own life. That was the moment I terrified myself. Who had I become? How had I lost myself so quickly?

I found satisfaction in the watching the blood drip from the point of the blade that had already pierced her flesh. She could no longer control herself. My own thoughts drowned out the sound of her cries as she pleaded for my help to stop her actions.

It was unnervingly intriguing. I wondered what it would look like to see more blood fall from her throat as the knife cut deeper.

Her eyes told of her complete and utter terror as she recognized the look of twisted pleasure on my face. The look in her eyes took me back to a moment I wanted to forget more than anything else in the world. It was the memory of being restrained on a bed with a man atop me and being made to watch the pleasure he took from my absolute terror was disgusting. Was I no better than him?

"No, stop it," I pleaded, but still reached for the brick of gold.

"Do you deny my offer?" The tempter straightened his posture. He looked down at me, eyes conveying his anger that I would even consider turning him down.

"I do. I can't let you hurt her." The moment I denied him, the solid form in my hand shifted back to its flaky state and slipped between my fingers. My heart sank to the bottom of my stomach as I watched it leave me.

"Well, that's disappointing. I guess I'll just have to do it myself then." He reached out, grabbed the girl, and pulled her to him. His hand covered hers as he forced her to press the knife deeper into her throat. She cried out from the pain and tears fell from her eyes.

"No!" I screamed and ran forward.

I pushed her away from the man, who caught me by my hair and wrapped his hands around my throat. He slammed me to the ground and held me in place; both thighs were a firm grip that locked against my waist.

"Get off." I choked out, but I could already feel the burn in my lungs from the struggle for air.

"You are weak, disgusting, and pathetic! I will enjoy this." He opened his mouth and out slid the split tipped tongue of a snake. He hissed at me and leaned closer to my face. "Delissscious," he spoke after his tongue slid across my flesh.

His jaw cracked as it unhinged and hung from his face, then his head slowly transformed from that of a man to that of a serpent. The pressure around my body tightened and I could just barely see that his legs had turned into a tail, even though his torso remained with arms and hands that still crushed my airways. This was it. The moment I would fail. I fought against him, but my body was weak, and his strength was inhuman.

He leaned in further and was just about as close as he could get to my face without touching me. He opened his mouth again to speak, but instead of the expected slow words with stretches on each syllable, there was a clicking noise followed by a gurgle and then blood spilled from his mouth and onto my face. His grip on my body from throat to legs slacked, and he fell to the ground beside me.

Erected at the back of his skull was the knife that he'd forced the girl to use on herself. The cloud lifted from my head just as a furious and exhausted Verena moved into view above me.

"You got your shit together yet, or do I have to turn this thing on you?" She wiped the blood from her collar and stared at me with eyes red with fury.

"No. Sorry, I don't know what got into me." I scrambled to get to my feet. I didn't want to give her any reason to believe she needed to worry about me turning on her again.

"It's the same thing that gets into everyone when faced with greed." She spit at the serpent. "He gets into your head and promises you that all of your desires will come true. All you have to do is sell him your soul."

The mountain of gold vanished, but the creepy body that was half man, half snake was still there. I kicked its outstretched hand away from me. What she said was true. From the moment my eyes saw that treasure, all I could think about was how much better and easier my life would be. All I really wanted was to live in peace. He'd offered me just that.

"Where is it?" I asked because I couldn't get past the feeling of hopelessness that had come over me.

"Where is what?" She leaned against a tree and tried to catch her breath. Her injuries were still severe. She should have been resting, not taking down some crazy magical serpent man.

"The gold, it was an enormous mountain of gold." Though I realized it was a test that I'd nearly failed, there was still a moment of disappointment.

"It never existed. He put that image in your head. That is what this place is. You need to remember that this is all just a big mind fuck designed to break you. Don't let it."

"I can't believe I almost let you kill yourself." The guilt of my actions became a knot in the pit of my stomach.

I'd never thought of myself as being capable of that degree of selfishness. Before my life changed, I'd never put someone else's safety beneath my own desire for an easier life. It scared me to see just how close I'd come to allowing that to happen. If I was capable of even that much, what else might I do?

"You didn't. You passed the test, and it's over now." Verena was being unusually understanding. If anything, I expected her to start straight in on chewing me a new one, but she was trying to comfort me in my moment of regret.

Thunder cracked over our heads as the clouds lit up seconds before rain poured down onto us. It was a light shower, but the approaching clouds indicated rougher weather would soon come.

"We need to find shelter and I need to tend to your wounds," I spoke to Verena, who simply nodded.

We stumbled through the trees for a short while and just as the sky opened to pour out its worst; we found a small cottage. It was quaint, yet eerie. The singular building was erected in the middle of nowhere on an island that no one knew existed. Yeah, no bad omens to worry about here!

I got the feeling that this place was bad news and it reminded me of the story of Hansel and Gretel. If it had been better conditions outside and Verena wasn't injured, I would have kept walking.

A cozy little nest in the trees sounded fantastic. Unfortunately, that alternative was not an option because we were both soaked from head to toe, and Verena could barely walk. I knocked on the door and waited for a response, but none came.

"Hello?" I knocked once more, and for good measure, called out to anyone that might dwell inside. Still, there was nothing.

Taking a chance, I tested the doorknob. When it turned, I looked to Verena who nodded. We were going inside. With a deep breath for courage and, even though my gut told me not to enter, I helped Verena cross the threshold.

CHAPTER 13

*W*e entered a home that was fully furnished and
ready for guests. I propped Verena up on the small
sofa and left her there to see if I could find anything to help us.
Aside from a few towels in a tiny bathroom, and a large blanket
that I pulled from the bed in the bedroom, there wasn't much.

What it had, however, was a working fireplace and a tall stack
of firewood, which I quickly got going. We undressed and hung
our clothing over chairs to dry and wrapped our bodies in the
towels and blanket. It surprised me to find that there were modern amenities that required electricity and plumbing. Both of
which I was sure the place didn't have given its isolated location.

The kitchen had jugs of drinking water inside of a small
refrigerator, which when I looked behind it, had no plug. There

wasn't even an electrical outlet on the wall. My curiosity quickly got the best of me. I was in a magical wonderland after all. Anything was possible.

I boiled some water over the fire because oddly there was no stove. Go figure! The warmed water was used to clean Verena's wounds before I dressed them. While walking through the woods, I gathered just enough ingredients to make one application of the salve. When the rain let up, I could go look for more. Verena carefully walked me through the process of making the ointment. Twice I thought I saw her smiling at my clumsy efforts.

The house had an intriguing device for water collection. The rain filtered in through a series of carefully placed holes in the roof and fell into various buckets that were attached to levers. When a bucket became full, the weight would cause it to drop and pull on the lever, which would then move a latch that sealed the hole above. It was really quite the ingenious design. I imagined the owner was an engineer of some sort. They would be someone who spent hours of each day tinkering away, creating new gadgets.

"I wonder who lives here." I looked around.

There wasn't much there, but there was enough to know that the owner cared for the place. It couldn't have been long since they were home. It was still pretty clean and everything functioned without issue.

"I don't care, as long as they don't catch us here." Verena winked and yawned. "They might not be so open to visitors even if they are two nude women."

"Maybe if we put on a little show for them." I puckered my lips and did a little shimmy that made Verena laugh.

"This place is pretty cozy, though. Glad we stumbled across it." She snuggled in deeper into the couch. "Nice not to have to sleep on the ground."

"Yeah, well, don't get too comfortable. We wouldn't want to wear out our welcome." As impressed as I was by the home, I still didn't feel completely comfortable being there.

"Of course not." She yawned and waved me off.

Eventually our clothes dried, and we redressed. I helped Verena, who was healing slowly. I told her I wanted to explore the home a bit more, and she nodded, curled up on the sofa and drifted off to sleep.

I went back to the bedroom, as it was the most interesting area in the home. I hoped I would find something that would provide insight about whoever owned the home. There was a small desk meant for writing. A half-melted candle, inkwell, and writing paper sat waiting on top. I hoped there would be some note written, something to give a clue about who lived there, but the paper was blank.

Based on the setting, I guessed the owner was the old-fashioned sort. Tattered curtains covered the windows, blocking out the moonlight. The sun had set and as the rain continued to pound against the roof; the moon rose and illuminated the night sky in its own incandescent glow.

There was a wardrobe opposite the desk. Inside it were a few jackets, which belonged to a man, and a locket hanging on a small hook inside the door. The locket held a faded picture of what looked like a woman. Of course, I stood there squinting and trying to decipher her features long enough to give myself a small headache. There was something more about it that captured my interest besides the mystery woman inside of the locket's casing.

The piece itself felt familiar in my hand. Holding it, I felt like I was home. It transported me back to my small apartment, to my sketchbook and junky coffee maker. I was safe and comfortable in my own bed.

The temptation to take it was strong. I wanted to keep that feeling forever. However, I thought better of it, and replaced it on the hook inside the door. It would be just my luck that it belonged to some oversized ogre of a man, and I'd walked away with the last memento of his one true love. I'd done enough running for my life as it was.

There wasn't much more to see. I lay across the bed, closed my eyes, and let my mind roam. What was Malachi up to? Was he okay? His smile, his scent, and his touch were all I could think of. I bit my lip as the memory of the sensation of his hands on my body stirred inside of me until they felt more tangible than a memory.

I gave into the feeling of his touch. I wanted so badly to be in his arms again. Eye still closed; my back arched from the bed as his lips trailed over my flesh. I wanted to experience him again. I froze when the zipper that kept my pants in place moved. Something or someone tugged on it.

"Malachi," I breathed his name as I opened my eyes and saw him on the bed beside me. He smiled before he devoured me in a kiss that stole away every breath I had left. "What are you doing here?" I gasped when he released my lips.

"Shh," he silenced me with a finger slightly pressed to my lips and continued his quest. Lips traveled across my body and left a small trail of heated expanses, which ignited so much more inside of me. My clothes were pulled away, and I lay there, bare against his already naked form. "Tell me you are mine," he requested. "I need to hear you say it."

I sighed and bit my lip. That request held so much meaning. I knew what he was really asking. He wanted me to bond with him. He wanted me to be his mate. This wasn't the first time the topic came up, and I was sure it wouldn't be the last.

"Say it, Sy." His begging was a soft rumble against my stomach.

"Malachi—" My mind was swimming with thoughts that were drowning in the flood of sensations caused by his touches. If he continued, I would agree to anything if only it meant that I could have him.

"Sy," he growled lowly. "You are mine, say it."

Just as I parted my lips, ready and willing to give him what he asked of me, just so that I could have more of him, another voice sounded from the corner. It was that same deep tone which belonged to a man that no longer existed. How often would I be haunted by the memory of him?

"She is not yours; she is mine," the voice proclaimed before he stepped forward from the shadows and smiled at me before turning his attention to his brother.

"She will never belong to you!" Malachi screamed and left me alone on the bed. He stood with his back to me, poised as if defending his territory.

"Yeah? We'll see about that." Demetrius lifted his hand to the charm that hung around his neck.

He ripped it away and tossed it to the floor at his feet. In a breath, man was no more and demon thrived. Terrifying and beautiful, he stepped forward and charged his brother. Malachi quickly side stepped his attacker before he removed his own charm and tossed it to me.

Two demons fought in front of me. Brothers ripped at one another for the sake of being able to claim me as their own. At first, I enjoyed the show of well-placed blows and even more skillful dodges. The sound of Demetrius' fist as it crashed into Malachi's jaw brought me back to reality.

These were my friends. They were people I cared about; their pain should never bring me entertainment or pleasure. They had helped me through so much, and yet I was just sitting aside and watching them fight for something I didn't want to give to either of them. My desire was to have them both, but that would never happen. To let them fight was cruel, and even though a part of me enjoyed it, I knew it was wrong.

"Stop!" I screamed repeatedly, but they ignored me. I had to act. Nothing about this was right. I jumped in between them, holding my hands against each of their chests. "Stop it! You are brothers. This is ridiculous. You have to stop fighting!"

"You must choose one of us," Demetrius said, and wrapped his hand around my waist, pulling me closer to him as if deciding for me.

"You must choose," Malachi repeated his brother's sentiment and echoed his movement.

There I stood, between the two of them, the one place I never wanted to be. I couldn't choose. I wouldn't. Both could stay with me, they could be with me forever. There was no need to choose. Their energy radiated and pulsated against my body.

Each breath I took filled my head with their rising pheromones and convinced me I could, in fact, have it all. I could keep them both with me. Demons became men again, and I wrapped my hands around the back of their necks and pulled each of them closer to me until their lips pressed against either side of my face and neck.

Though my call should not have affected them in such an intense way, I could see my power roll over them as it coerced the two men into fulfilling my selfish desires. They were under my influence and my wants controlled their actions. Instead of fighting each other, they switched their focus to bringing me pleasure.

Malachi knelt in front of me and kissed my stomach, while Demetrius stood behind me and caressed my breasts. Hands touched my body, and I moaned in pleasure as Malachi's lips wrapped around my nipples and Demetrius fell to his knees behind me. He kissed the small of my back as his hand slipped in between my thighs. He coaxed the first orgasm from me before Malachi lifted me from my feet and placed me on the bed.

CHAPTER 14

It was difficult to keep track of who did what to my body. Warm lips wrapped around my nipple as a thick tongue delved between my legs and hands continued to roam my body. My hands alternated between clutching dreads, rubbing smooth scalp, stroking dick, and pulling at the sheets that covered the mattress.

Over and over, I cried out in orgasm as they worked to please me. This was what I wanted. I didn't have to choose I could have them both.

"Demetrius?" The annoying familiarity of the voice that dared to interrupt my pleasure instantly angered me.

"Get out!" I yelled at Verena, who stood by the door with a look of shock on her face.

"What the hell is this?" she stared at us with disgust.

"I told you to leave." I moved from the bed and my lovers stayed in their place and waited for my return.

"This is sick. They are brothers!" She yelled, pointing to the bed. "What the hell is wrong with you?"

"Why do you care?" I pointed at the door, giving her one final warning. "Get out!"

"You can't do this!" She looked past me to Demetrius and tears fell from her eyes. "This isn't right."

I looked to the bed, anger bubbling in my belly. Why did she look at him like that? Why did she care so much? He belonged to me. They both did.

"Why can't I have them both?" I returned to the bed to stroke each of their faces, paying extra attention to the older brother. Both rewarded me with a smile that told me they were happy with our arrangement. "Look at them, they are mine!"

"Demetrius?" she said again and stepped closer to the bed. He looked at her with a blank stare. How did they know each other?

"Don't talk to him!" I jumped from the bed again and pushed her. Her back slammed into the wall.

"You can't have him!" she yelled at me and despite her injuries, she charged at me.

It was then my turn to wrestle across the room. After being with Malachi and Demetrius, I was rejuvenated. Even after climbing from the bed, their energy still fed my own. Verena, with her injuries, didn't stand a chance against me, but we still fought. We tumbled around the bedroom.

Verena was the skilled siren, but she was no fighter. Each time we met, I knocked her back, but she kept up her aggression. The third time she charged me; I caught her by the throat, lifted her from her feet, and slammed her to the ground. My grip tightened, and I growled. It was my turn to protect what was mine.

"They are mine!" I lifted her and slammed her again into the floor. Her eyes rolled into the back of her head for a moment, but she was still conscious.

"Choose. You have to choose." She spit blood into my face and turned her head to look at Demetrius before she vanished. Though she was gone, I still heard her warning. "You can't have them both."

Confused, I searched the room. What kind of magic was she wielding? How was she gone? I looked at the bed; two brothers sat staring in wait, completely under my control. The joy I felt only lasted a moment before the sharp pain in my stomach forced me to double over.

I clutched myself and fell to the floor. I expected them to run to me and try to help me after they watched me double over. Unfortunately, they were useless because my magic still trapped them.

Help me!" I called to them but neither moved. "Please."

"You must choose." The shrill trill of the naiad's voice echoed. The meaning of her words was now clear to me.

"Why is everyone so hell bent on my choosing? Why do I have to choose?" I tried to stand, but the discomfort forced me back down to the floor.

"A mated siren is a siren who knows loyalty. She is one who can be trusted. She is one who will not bring harm to innocent men." The nymph spoke and once again, she didn't allow me to see her face. I was sure she was without the illusion of beauty because of the sharp stabbing sensation that lingered in my ear at the end of every word.

"I don't want to choose." I stared at the brothers and could do nothing to hold back my tears. "It's not fair. I never wanted any of this, and now you are forcing me to hurt one of them."

"You must choose," she repeated her command and left me no choice. There would be no moving forward in my task if I didn't decide. That much was obvious. Why else would the naiad be so concerned with who I chose as my mate?

The pain receded allowing me to return to my feet. What I had to do was impossible, but I did it. I made my choice. I fell into the arms of the brother I wanted most and buried my face against his chest. My tears continued to fall as the other disappeared and tried not to see the hurt that painted his expression.

When I opened my eyes, I was lying in a field. Tall grass wafted around me. My protectors were both gone. The small house with its ingenious water collection system had vanished and Verena made no reappearance. The man whose chest I laid on had also disappeared. I was completely alone.

"It is time," the voice of the naiad sounded from every direction.

"Time for what, what do you want me to do?" I asked, as I wiped away residual tears.

"You must climb Mt. Ononolo and if you have what it takes to make it to the top, you can have your stone, and the power it represents," she said, sounding upset that I had made it this far.

"What about all the challenges I was supposed to face?" Of course, I didn't want things to continue, but it didn't seem as if I had done anything much outside of run for my life.

"You have completed your task." Once again, she sounded more disappointed than anything else. This woman wanted me to fail. It was no surprise after the way I had insulted her.

"You proved your compassion for others when you helped a fallen stranger who had no way to repay you for your kindness. You could have left her behind, but you didn't, even though it was a burden on your progress. You put the welfare of another above your own.

"You proved you were brave when you fought to save your guide. There was no guarantee either of you would survive, and yet you faced a beast also unknown to you to save her life. The test of your spirit proved a tough one and yet you excelled.

"You overcame the sticky hold of greed. You turned down the chance of having your every wish come true, once again showing your compassion for others and that you can see outside of yourself.

"You proved by choosing a mate to bond with that your lust for men is not one that will easily overwhelm you. Though you had to inevitably hurt someone close to you, your decision was for the greater good.

"This stage is the ultimate challenge. It is the test of your endurance, your commitment, your determination, and your will to make it through."

The smell of burning earth overwhelmed me and turned around to find the volcano, the same one I'd seen in my dreams. The top glowed in a red halo and smoke rose from its mouth. I could only imagine what it would be like at the peak. How was I supposed to make it to the top of an active volcano? I thought she would say more, offer me words of advice, but she did not.

At the base of Ononolo, everything was calm. Besides the scent of burning lands that drifted down from the top of the rising, there was nothing. I checked my body, suddenly aware of the vulnerable position I'd been put in, and sighed. Relieved, I found myself completely clothed. I took a moment to hype myself up and began my hike.

Not long into my climb did I smell the gas. The odor was nauseating. It seeped through the cracks in the ground. Initially, it was just the smell that bothered me, but soon the headache began. After that, as I pushed my way toward the top and the terrain became more difficult to traverse. My vision blurred and everything I saw doubled. I stumbled as a wave of vertigo washed over me.

The first time I fell, I blinked, and the world changed. I was just a baby again. Staring up through virgin eyes, I saw a woman whose smile read of the unconditional love she held for her newborn daughter. My small hand with stubby fingers wrapped around her finger and I could hear myself cooing as she spoke my name and told me she loved me.

I shook the hallucination away and continued. The next stumble landed me on my ass, and as I attempted to get up, the rush of blood to my head sent me back to the same room, a baby once again. The only change was that it was a man who held me. He dangled a locket in front of me and told me it belonged to me. His face was completely unfamiliar, but I could tell in his eyes that he was my father. No one else had ever looked at me like that; it was undeniable.

The visions from that point forward continued in an endless rotation of images that refused to release me. My body weakened as I continued to climb the side of the volcano. Sheer will and determination kept my limbs pushing forward. After all I had gone through, there was nothing that would stop me from seeing this through to the end. Even though my path was barely visible as I moved between hallucinations.

I blinked, and I was lying on my back as a man propped himself above me. His face, unlike that of my father's, I would never forget. My hands and legs were bound, and I struggled beneath him. I tried to remind myself that the vision was a lie. I had escaped that horrible place and none of what I was being forced to witness him do to my body was happening, no matter how real it felt.

Moments of the past months flashed in my mind, some accurate, some not. Men who I had encountered all ended up dead even though I knew I'd left them alive. Malachi shifted from being my caring lover and protector to my abuser. I reminded myself that he'd never hit me once. He would never hurt me that way.

The smell of gas slowly diminished as the wind picked. The fresh air helped to keep the visions away. Without the hallucinations I was able to make actual progress. Hours passed, and I continued to climb. Exhaustion crippled me, as the energy I pulled from my entanglement with the Denali brothers faded.

Often I would lose consciousness. My eyes closed with the sun bearing down on me and opened to the night sky. I would pass out and wake to the sun burning into my flesh. The rotation of the celestial tracks above me was the only thing that gave me any sign of how long I'd been climbing. The smoke from the volcano blocked out the moon and stars, but conveniently moved in the opposite direction and allowed the damaging rays of the sun full access to my dehydrated body.

I slept through bouts of rain, which were just enough to keep my body from turning into a raisin. It wasn't as good as being submerged in the ocean, but it worked just as well to give me some strength back. I opened my mouth to drink the water, which made my stomach hurt but was better than the pain of dehydration.

As the top came into view, I had a moment of exhilaration. The hot halo meant my agony was nearly over. Then the volcano erupted. It spit out streams of lava and balls of fire, which I initially dodged, but eventually my body seized from fatigue. With the first hit of flesh searing pain, it was all I could do not to pass out.

The moment the fire touched my skin, the flesh burned and melted away, leaving open wounds. On my arms and thighs, the heat burned right through the layers of fabric that tried to protect my skin, and the shoes that I was so happy to have in the jungle melted and fused with my feet as I trudged on. My cries were endless but I continued.

The mouth of the volcano was now within my view. A ray of hope, but my legs had become useless and the small clear paths that I had navigated had all but disappeared, which meant more burns and increased pain. My head spun, and I tripped and landed in ash and embers that seared the flesh of my face.

The tears that fell from my eyes stung when they met the open wounds on my face. Still, I crawled to the edge and what I saw made my heart flutter. It was there, my stone. It floated in the center of the mouth of the volcano, far out of reach. I pulled myself to my knees, dropped my head back, and screamed into the sky. *How the hell was I supposed to reach it?* Ononolo rumbled beneath me and the lava that remained inside of it bubbled up. Soon it would fully erupt and eliminate any hope I had of getting my stone.

With my last stores of strength, I stood. I gagged as I looked down at my legs. My bones were now showing as the flesh and much of the muscle in my legs had dissolved from the heat. I had one chance to do this. There wouldn't be another, I wouldn't survive it.

The jump that sent me forward into the fire broke the bones in my right leg. I cried, but used the pain to push me forward. With my hand stretched as far as it would go, I reached for my stone. Just before I touched it, my fingers inches away, the volcano erupted and the flames consumed my body.

CHAPTER 15

There is no other feeling that quite compares to that of warm sand against your skin. My eyes were still closed, but I could hear the waves crashing nearby, and the mist of salty water sprayed across my skin. The moments of rejuvenation as it cooled my flesh from the heat of the sun were pure bliss.

My stomach knotted as the memory of what I'd just gone through registered. My body had to be covered from head to toe in blisters. I expected pain across every inch of my body where there should be bruises, broken bones, and sites of missing flesh. Refusing to open my eyes, I waited with each passing moment for the onslaught of pain.

I knew it would happen once the adrenaline wore off. The moments continued and still there was just the warmth of the sun and the misty breezes of ocean air. I dared to open my eyes and hoped the sensations I felt weren't just another cruel delusion forced on me. I stared at the sky for a moment, trying to remember the specifics of what happened.

I remembered my climb, the visions, the stone, and tossing myself into the mouth of the volcano, hoping to reach it. Then there was nothing at all for a long time, and I was completely aware of the nothingness. My consciousness was still active, even though there was nothing for it to process. It disconnected me from my physical self. It felt a lot like what I imagined dying would feel like. Nothingness that stretched on infinitely until even that small bit of my consciousness that truly made me myself faded away. I waited for the fadeout.

Eventually, the fear of false security passed, and I thought it best to get up. The spot was comfortable, but I had to figure out what was next so I could attempt to get home. My vertical position revealed that I had been lying near the water's edge. Nearby were clusters of large rocks that sat in the water being pounded by the waves.

The call of the ocean was much stronger than it had ever been. Like a lasso wrapping around me, it pulled me towards the shallow depths. The water called to me; my home called to me. My legs carried me forward, and my heart raced with each step.

Standing atop one of the large rocks, I looked out into the blue span, but the flicker of red fabric caught my attention. A crimson dress, the same shade of deep red as my tail, flowed around me. It felt symbolic as it trailed behind me, being pushed and lifted by the wind.

The water swelled, spraying my body, and submerging my feet in the high wave. I smiled as the energy pulled into my body from the water. This was nothing like I'd experienced ever before. I wanted to rip the dress from my body and dive beneath the coming wave.

As I contemplated jumping into the water, I realized my hand was clutched around something hard and round. I opened my palm to reveal the stone, the one I'd been reaching for when everything went black. It seemed so inaccessible, and yet there it was. Small, smooth stone with a slight pink tint. I held it between my fingertips as I inspected it. It glowed slightly, and I felt a pulse of energy move from it to me.

I did it! I'd succeeded! I got my stone!

After my quick moment of celebration, I turned away from the ocean. There was still so much to do, and getting back to Malachi was a top priority. The island was familiar, at least. It was the same one I had washed up on after rescuing Verena from the monster who used her as bait.

I walked along the same path. A new feeling of instinct drove my momentum. Unlike the last time I left the beach side, I was in full control of my actions. I was under no spell. I tested the theory to be sure and stopped mid-stride to turn and go in an alternate direction.

It worked, but the feeling in my stomach told me I needed to go back. Whatever happened next in my journey was on that path. Each step seemed familiar. Each step had a purpose and when I realized where I was headed, my stomach filled with butterflies of nerves and fear.

This time, the small house was active. Smoke billowed up from the chimney and light shone from within. The owner, whoever he or she may be, was home. A light tap on the door pushed it open and the screech of its hinges announced my presence to the man who stood with his back to me. My hand clutched the door frame as my breath halted.

"Syrinada," he said my name as he turned to me and his face brought back memories I hadn't realized were with me. Memories of a man who loved me, a man who promised the world to both my mother and me.

"You're—" the words wouldn't cross my lips. I couldn't call this man my father. I didn't even know him.

"Finally, you've come to me, my daughter." He smiled, and I felt his happiness radiate to me. This man was my father. There was no doubt in my mind.

"This is your home?" I couldn't believe I had just been there touching the possessions of my own father and hadn't known I'd been so close to him. No, I wouldn't think about sitting naked on his couch or the jokes made about him, the owner, being pleased to find me that way. *Gross.*

"Well, it's something like that. Your mother and I used this place for our rendezvous. Its hidden from both sides of our family. Our magic combined, created a cloaking spell that would keep us safe here. It is where our love blossomed and turned into something beautiful." He pointed at me. "You."

"I thought you were dead." I blurted out.

I hated to follow up such a sweet sentiment with such a harsh topic, but I had a million and one things I wanted to say and questions to ask, and that was number one. Where had he been? He frowned as he thought about my outburst and I waited for his response.

"No, far from it, in fact. I am very much alive." He spread his arms out and displayed himself as physical proof.

"Why are you here? Why am I? Where have you been all this time?" The questions spewed out of my mouth and all he did was smile at me again.

"I'm here to claim you, my daughter. It wasn't possible before this moment because they hid you from me. I had to wait until you got your stone; it was the only way to break the spell your aunt commissioned."

"Noreen did this? Hid me from you?" Anger warmed my belly as I considered what he said. "why would she do that?"

After all that I knew of my aunt, all that I had found out, and all that she had already done to me, his revelation didn't shock me. Yet another misfortune in my life seemed to be caused by her hand. I could only wonder how much more would prove to be rooted back to her.

"I wish I could give you an explanation. I have been exerting myself for years, trying to figure out the answer to that question. Noreen never seemed to like me that much." He scratched his the small goatee on his chin. "Maybe she wanted to punish me. She could have also blamed me for your mother's death and wanted to keep you away from me.

"I've considered the possibility that it was your mother's wish to keep you safe from my people. Whatever the reason, I remain in the dark. What I do know is that for the longest time, I have been searching for you. I could never find you. Even though I knew she had you cloaked from me, I still tried. I never stopped trying. How could I ever give up on you? You are my daughter."

"Well, here I am." I held my arms out as if putting myself on display.

He took that as an invitation for a hug and scooped me up into his arms. My heart paused for a moment as his embrace tightened around me. The feeling was unreal, oddly unwanted, but also everything that I never knew I had been missing out on.

"Yes, here you are." He put me back down, holding me at arm's length, and a proud smile stretched across his face.

"I have a weird question for you, but it's one I've never been given an answer to." I paused for a moment because it really made me feel silly to ask. "What is your name?"

He chuckled as if he'd expected as much. "My name is Alderic. It causes me such heartache to know that you were not told much of me. Perhaps that is something that we can rectify now. I would love to get to know you."

I looked at Alderic, really looked at him for the first time without the overwhelming pulsing of my heart to distract me. He looked nothing as I'd imagined him the few times I pictured what my father could look like.

His skin was darker than mine was, which explained why my skin was a deeper tone than that of my aunt's. She would sunbathe for days to reach my natural complexion. He was from New Orleans. This much I knew from the short bit Malachi told me of him. His brown skin and crooked smile with the slow drawl of his words fit perfectly. It became impossible not to stare at him. Luckily, he didn't seem to mind it.

He had been a major missing piece of my life. He'd gone on talking about the house, how he took pride in crafting it for my mother. His honey tinted eyes lit up and danced whenever he mentioned her and I loved it. To be loved like that even long after you're gone is the kind of love people dream about. My mother had that with this man. I hoped in some way she could still feel it.

He was also shorter than I imagined, but I figure every little girl imagines her father to stand towers above the world, whereas he was just about five inches taller than I was. I took as much of him in as I could. Breathed in the scent of his cologne. It was a deep sort of sweetness that I couldn't place but loved.

Once or twice, I got this urge to hug him again, to wrap my arms around his neck, and just hang there. Having never experienced his embrace prior to that day, nothing would have been better. Instead, I kept my arms to myself in various positions, either by my side, wrapped around my torso or folded behind my back. All my fidgeting no doubt informed him of just how nervous I was.

"I would like for you to come with me Syrinada." His face held a proud yet questioning expression.

"Come with you, where?" There was that sting of instinct in my gut, but the meaning behind it was unclear.

"To my home." He answered as if it were obvious.

"I thought this was your home." I looked around the small place again.

"This, no, not at all." He laughed. "This place was just for your mother. I only come from time to time to make sure it still stands and to remember better times." A more somber expression replaced the smile, one that I couldn't stand to see.

"Why do you want me to come with you?" The pang in my stomach intensified, and it worried me. Was I not supposed to accept this offer?

"There is so much you don't know, so much that I can teach you. The world is about to change for you in such a drastic way. Who better to show you how to navigate it than I?"

"I'm not sure if I should. Malachi and the others, they're waiting for me." I took a step back.

He winced when I backed away from him. As if my considered rejection caused him physical pain. And of course, this made me feel like the dirt under the house. I didn't want to hurt him, but something about his offer didn't feel right.

"Syrinada, I have waited for you for your entire life. I know you have your ties to your friends, but I won't keep you away for long. I'm sure they can wait a short time." His pleading eyes met my apprehensive ones, and I sighed.

What was I supposed to do? Was I supposed to tell this man, that my gut told me he wasn't worthy of my trust? If it weren't for him, I wouldn't even exist.

"I don't know," I hesitated.

With a look of determination, he turned and headed down the hall, pausing only to wait for me to follow him. We entered the bedroom, and I tried my best to think of anything other than what I'd done in my parents' bed.

He swung the doors of the wardrobe open and searched the interior. Whatever was inside, he felt it would convince me to change my mind. From the hook, he lifted the locket, the same one I'd held in my hand the last time I was there and handed it to me.

"Put it on, we always meant it to be yours."

I pulled the chain over my neck. The cool metal pulsed against my skin. I lifted the locket, and the clasp glowed with a light that peeked from within. When I opened it, the picture that was faded the last time was renewed, and my mother's face appeared, smiling back at me.

On the other side was something I hadn't noticed before. A baby, a chubby little girl with bright eyes, and a wide toothless smile. It was me. I couldn't help the smile that spread across my face or the tears that fell from my eyes. I had never received a more precious gift.

I looked up at Alderic who smiled again. He turned, pushed on the back panel of the wardrobe, and stepped aside. It split in half, revealing a doorway of light. My father, a man who was a stranger to me, held his hand out to me.

"Come with me my daughter."

With reluctance, I went against that nagging feeling in my gut and placed my hand in his. Together we walked into the light.

CHAPTER 16

I'd expected to cross the threshold and find myself in a place that would exhilarate me with its magical whim. I'd expected a mansion or a castle, Hogwarts style with dragons flying in the distance. What I got was a large open field and a small two-story house.

There was no magic or any display of excessive grandeur. It looked like we were in the back hills of the country, whose country I did not know, since grass and a sparse assortment of trees were all that I could see.

"This is home." Alderic waved his hands out in front of us, proud of his abode.

"It's nice." I tried not to let on that I was a little disappointed.

"I know it's not much from the outside," he laughed. "But what lies beneath its surface will amaze you."

The walk to the house was an awkward one. What do you say to the man who, although he was your father, was a complete and total mystery? What conversation piece was adequate? Instead of trying for small talk, we walked in silence.

All the excitement and the motivation to talk that I had before we crossed the threshold dissipated, and it left me without words. Guilt crept over me because, had it been my mother beside me, I would have a million questions at the ready. I'd rehearsed so many conversations with her. If it had been my mother, I'd have been talking her ear off about all the things I wished she could have been around for.

That was a moment I had been dreaming about my entire life, but sad to say, though I often wondered about him, I never longed for my father in the same way I did my mother. I wondered about him, but as I grew older, I accepted his absence because in my mind; it was a choice he made. It wasn't the same for her. They took her life from her; he chose to live his away from me.

From the only brief description of Alderic my aunt Noreen provided, he didn't seem to be someone I would really care about knowing. I hoped the way I felt would change, that it was all still a part of the magic Noreen had woven to keep us apart. I wasn't sure; but it wasn't too farfetched to believe that magic could alter thoughts and emotions?

It was just as Verena had told me; anything was indeed possible, even if it was morally corrupt. Besides, if a siren could make a man leave his entire life, it couldn't be that outrageous of an idea that the magic of a witch could make it so that a daughter wouldn't long for her father.

We made it to the door, and he placed a key in the large lock. Why he needed to lock a home that sat in the middle of nowhere, I would never understand. Perhaps he got more unwanted visitors than one would imagine, though I couldn't see what a standard lock would do if a coven of witches came to your front door.

"Are you ready?" He noticed how intently I'd been staring at the key. "I like the novelty of it." He shrugged.

Well, that was one mystery solved.

"Yeah, I guess." I shrugged.

I had come that far. What would be the point of not seeing it through? At least I wanted to. The pangs in my gut had ceased, and I took the relief as a positive sign.

The key turned and the sound of bolts and locks reversing their direction rang out. One key operated what sounded like fifty security bolts, revealing that there was a bit more than just novelty to the function. When the last one sounded, the door opened and revealed complete wonder.

My jaw damn near hit the floor when I saw the inside of Alderic's home. The simple exterior of the two story home was a total illusion. Instead of a homey interior with worn couches and dusty countertops, the door opened to reveal a modern design with rustic contemporary finishes. It was smooth, stylish, and much larger than should have been physically possible. The house seemed to expand with each step I took inside.

"How is this even possible?" I stepped back onto the porch to do a double take and yes, the house still looked like the same quaint little country home.

"Magic of course." He smiled. "This is my home. And yours temporarily, as long as you choose to remain here."

My father walked me through the halls of his stunning home and proudly told me of the work he put into creating it. He spent countless hours building both with magic and manual labor. The interior was immaculate. Modern pieces set sparingly around the home. Each one possessed its own touch of industrialized markings. There were rounded chairs and sofas with large metal hinges and bolts as accents.

Everything was done in grays, blacks, and muted reds. My favorite piece had to be the large coffee table. It was the only piece that matched nothing else in the home. The wooden table had three wheels locked in place that functioned as its legs. I imagined this was a gift, one he couldn't part with for sentimental reasons. Maybe my mother had given it to him. It was comforting to think about.

This home fit the man who acted as my tour guide. If I could see the inner workings of his mind, I imagined it would look much like the home he created. In corners, there were pieces of pure magnificence that exuded the magic he possessed. Exotic plants bowed to me and giggled as I walked by. Some seemed to sing my name in a melody that was barely above a whisper.

Painted pictures with changing images lined the walls. The paint shifted to display images I could only assume were meant to be pleasing to the current viewer. One held a picture of the two of us. We'd never posed for it, but there we were, a father with his arm around his daughter's shoulders. Both of us smiled. It looked promising, a glimpse of possible things to come.

"It's so beautiful here." My voice echoed off the high ceiling as we climbed the stairs.

He pointed off to one end, "My bedroom is this way."

He then ushered me in the opposite direction. We passed two other bedrooms with closed doors, which he didn't bother to open, and finally landed at the end of the hall. He pushed a set of double doors open to reveal a room staged for a daughter.

Bright shades of pink and purple, and all the frilly stuff a girl should like, overwhelmed the room. The bed, which sat in the center of the room, overflowed with fluffy pillows and teddy bears. The décor was not at all what I would have ever chosen for myself. I smiled because I could tell it meant so much to him. He really tried. This room, though meant for me, was not really my own, so it didn't matter the color scheme. I wouldn't be there long.

"I hope you like it." Alderic smiled as he adjusted one of the stuffed bears.

"It looks cozy." I lied.

After showing me the upstairs, we headed for the basement, which turned out to be a massive underground lair. He designed the space for the sole purpose of being used as a training facility. We didn't get too deep into details because a strange buzzing sound came from the ring he wore on his finger. With a frustrated sigh, he apologized for needing to leave my side.

"I'll be back as soon as I can." He promised and twisted the ring on his finger ending the buzzing. "I'm sorry about this."

"It's fine. I can just roam around here if that's okay." I wanted to see what the gym had to offer.

"Of course." He hugged me quickly before leaving me alone.

I assured him again that I would be okay and could remember my way around. Honestly, I was happy about his distraction. It gave me time alone to process my thoughts. How was it I was now in my father's home? Had I made the wrong decision to go with him? Things were happening so fast and I needed time to think without him there to cloud my judgment. It was hard to be skeptical when he kept smiling as if he'd won the lottery. I didn't want to take that away from him.

Alone in the basement, I walked around but refrained from touching anything. I was afraid of any magic booby traps that I might trigger. What the hell would I do if I tripped and landed on something that turned me into a toad? Ah, wouldn't that be nice! I'm sure it would solve many of my issues. Hell, who would feel threatened by me then?

I found myself in a room void of many objects. It had the artificial glow of a sun that didn't exist below the surface. The room itself felt like a welcoming hug, a friend eager to meet me and hear all my woes. I sat down on the circular sofa in the middle of the room. Leaned my head back and relaxed.

I couldn't remember the last time I'd truly had a moment of tranquility. In that room, it seemed that was all I could do. Perhaps that was the purpose of it. After a long day of brutal training, one would get to go there and allow the calming aura to wash over them. I looked forward to spending more time in this room, though I hadn't planned on extending my stay for much longer. This would need to be a quick visit, and then I had to get back to reality, and to my friends.

"Hello." A smooth voice echoed through the room.

It quickly replaced my sense of serenity with a rush of excitement. Who was he, and how could I know everything about him? I took a moment to get a hold of myself before I turned to meet the unfamiliar presence. I was the siren, after all. How would it look if I was fumbling over some random guy?

I turned to find a man who was simply put, delicious. Skin a deep shade of hickory covered his tall, muscular frame. The cool smile and chestnut eyes called to my darker side. This man was a natural intoxication. He only needed to say hello and my head was spinning. In that moment, I could tell that if given the chance, he would have me in the palm of his hand and I would never want to leave.

"Hello," My reply was a struggle which only became more difficult when he gave me another flash of his wide smile.

"My name is Rhys." He bit his bottom lip and looked over the length of my body. "You must be, Syrinada."

"Yes." I nodded. "It's nice to meet you, Rhys."

He approached me, crossing the room with long strides. I watched each step that carried him closer to me and wished his legs would move faster.

"What are you doing here? Are you working for my father?" I hated how suspicious I sounded, but hell, I was. This man looked like my own damn brand of kryptonite. He had to be up to no good.

He laughed at my raised eyebrow and offered his explanation easily. "You could say that. He is my mentor."

"A mentor, for magic?" What the hell else would it be? I wanted to run and hit a reset button and start the conversation over!

"Yes, it's something usually done by a father, but mine passed away when I was a young boy. Alderic has always been close to my family and though he was an outcast to our people, my mother kept in touch with him. She trusted him. As she put it, her opinion was the only one that mattered. When I turned eighteen, she sent me here to be with him."

"How long have you been here?" I asked, ignoring the feeling of jealousy that crept up inside of me.

"Years. Let's see, I'm twenty-eight now, so just over a decade."

"Do you ever get to leave? I mean, it's gorgeous here but, do you ever get to explore the world outside?"

"When I first got here, no, but that was because I was too inexperienced. One false move could have cost him everything. I hated it, but I understood his reasons. I'm not sure what my mom told everyone to explain my absence, but no one ever came looking for me. Now I come and go as I please," he smiled. "How long do you plan on staying here?"

"I'm not really sure. He said he wanted to train me, teach me things about magic that my friends back home cannot." How long would that take? I didn't have a decade to give to him. Perhaps he would let me do as Rhys did, and I could come and go as I pleased. That would be the only way I would agree to stay.

"He spoke of you often. During my time here, I have heard so many stories about you. I'm not sure if he told you, but he kept watch over you through magic. Before they took you from him, he performed a series of spells that would allow him to know that you were okay. The spells he put in place when you were a baby still worked, and although he couldn't see you, he could feel you.

"Whenever you were in danger, hurt, or afraid, he could use those ties to send you help or energy to keep you going. It was hard to watch some days. His frustration, his disappointment, his torment. I wondered how much longer he could go on. He wanted nothing more than to find you.

"Some days I could take his mind off it. I could use magic to give him something else to focus on. Unfortunately, that didn't always work and there were times when it made matters worse because I could tell he wished it were you he was working with instead of me."

"Wow." I looked around the room and sighed. "Honestly, I never expected him to care."

"Why wouldn't you think your father cared about you?"

"The things I was told about my father." I shook my head. "My aunt made him out to be selfish and unkind. I knew he loved my mother, but I was never sure what else to believe. This is insane. I mean, In the past few weeks, I've found out that so much about my life has been a lie."

"That must be difficult, living with the wool pulled over your eyes."

"Tell me about it." I laughed. "I actually think the wool was just fine. It's having it removed that sucks."

"Can I offer you a bit of advice? We don't know each other at all, so you can tell me to shut up and I'll respect that."

"I'll take whatever advice I can get now." What could it hurt?

"Enjoy this time. I would do anything to have a second chance with my father." Rhys spoke honestly. "Let go of whatever you were told about him, the good and the bad, and make your opinions for yourself."

"That is actually really good advice, and I'm sorry about your dad."

"Thanks." He clapped his hands. "Now, let's get to work."

"What?" I stared at him. What work did he expect me to be doing?

"Your father has requested that I spend some time with you to work on basic techniques. I believe he thinks it will help build your confidence as well as lessen the intimidation factor when you finally get to work one on one with him."

"So no buffer time huh, right to business?" I shook my head.

"Well, that's just one more lesson about dear old dad that you can use to decide how you feel about him." He chuckled and winked at me.

Dear god, how was I supposed to focus on anything with this man as my tutor?

"Your magic is different." Rhys started after leading me to the training floor.

"Different in what way?"

"Its more internal, focused. Most witches require aids, talismans, symbols that feed their power. Others require incantations, spells. While you can do spell work, you are not the same as other witches. You don't require those things to make your magic work."

"Do you have one? A talisman, I mean."

"Yea, and maybe I'll tell you what it is someday." He winked. "Its not something easily divulged."

"Oh," I smiled. "I hope you can trust me with that one day."

"Yeah," he nodded. "Instead of focusing on the talisman, you will have to look within yourself. Feel the power that thrives in your blood and channel that energy."

"Right, sounds simple enough."

"Are you ready to begin?"

"No time like the present, right?" I shrugged. What else was I going to do with my time?

Training was an alternation of a vast array of experiences, ranging from pleasant surprises to near torture. The sessions with Rhys were intense and left me feeling like my body would collapse into itself, a total implosion. He pulled no punches and pushed me far beyond my limits.

There were plenty of times that I felt ready to walk away. Yet every time the words bubbled to the surface, I became overwhelmed with a growing need to make him proud. I wanted to show him I could take anything he threw at me.

I told myself my obsession was rooted in my need for Rhys to give Alderic a good review. Then I realized it was more than that. Just like the white room, Rhys used magic to adjust my mood. Instead of calming me, it made me eager and more aggressive.

When I worked out what was happening, I wasn't mad about it. I learned so much and the need to continue became a natural impulse. No magical induction required. Yet still, often I would have to crawl back to my bed, tired, sore, and happy to fall into the nauseating pink and purple fluff that waited.

It wasn't until the third day that I worked with my father, and I learned that the two men were completely different in training. Once we were in the training room, my dear old dad vanished and the drill sergeant from hell took his place. I thought of just throwing in the towel, waving the white flag, and moving on with my life. Nowhere in his invitation for this father daughter time had he expressed that if it I accepted; it would be equal to enlisting in the damn army.

With Rhys, I had fun. He was tough, but he also took the time to ensure that every task he set reminded me of just how much pleasure could come in learning to conjure. My father however, attempted to cram years of lessons into a short time, resulting in the slow growth of my loathing for the experience.

Rhys wanted me to remember that magic was something to be enjoyed, no matter how terrible and draining learning it was turning out to be. All that I needed to remember was that in the end, it would be worth it.

Something I didn't express to Rhys was that my father often frightened me. I didn't want to seem ungrateful. It just seemed rude to complain about my dad when he didn't have one. Rhys never witnessed the intensity of Alderic when he showed his anger and frustration that I wasn't where he wanted me to be.

He kept our sessions private because he didn't want me to lose focus. It was as if he had a deadline that he wasn't sharing with me. I didn't understand what the big deal was, but to him, I had to be perfect. And I was far from it.

"You have to be better than this, Syrinada." Alderic barked at me. "Focus."

"I'm doing my best." I responded and collapsed on the floor. "I'm tired."

"Your enemy will never tire. They will come at you one hundred times stronger than this." He walked circles around me. "Do you expect them to wait while you catch your breath?"

"Look, I appreciate this, the training, the education, but this is too much."

"How disappointing." Alderic turned his back on me to head to the door. "I had such high hopes for you. I guess I was wrong."

He left me sitting in a puddle of my own sweat and reconsidering my decision to come to his home. If he was so disappointed with me, he wouldn't care if I left.

My time spent with Rhys made it easier to get through the intense time with the old man. Whenever Alderic made me want to scream, I would remember that my next session would be with Rhys. It would be easier because of his calm, guiding hand. Time seemed to pass too quickly whenever I was with him. I learned a lot, but often found it difficult to focus on my tasks.

His smile was intoxicating, and his touch was exciting. Everything about him woke up something more inside of me, and the part of me that flourished beneath the seas would surface. I had to remind myself that I was there to learn, not to be drooling over some guy, no matter how hot, sweet, and caring he was. Rhys was off limits to me. He had to be.

The fifth day we worked together, he taught me how to move the air around me and wield it to do whatever I wished. Over and over, he pushed and lifted me with a gentle movement. When I tried to do the same, I smashed him against a wall then flattened him on the floor.

No matter how many times my efforts ended in his pain, Rhys would laugh and tell me I was improving. When the same thing happened with my father, he yelled and left me alone in the room to practice on a chair. Eventually, I mastered the skill, but it was clear at that point that I would spend more time wishing I hadn't gone home with Alderic.

CHAPTER 17

After one of our tougher training sessions, Rhys requested I accompany him to his quarters. It was a part of the house my father hadn't shown me. At the far end of the basement, opposite where we'd entered, was another door. It opened a second house of sorts. This was Rhys' home.

"How have I never noticed this?" I eyed the door, then scanned our surrounding. Was there more that I'd missed about the space?

"It's hidden, for a reason." He winked.

"What are we doing here? Not that I mind a change of scenery." The magic of the home, which initially interested me, had become boring. There were only so much giggly plants and moving pictures a girl could take before it all became monotonous.

"I want to make something for you, something I think you need." Rhys left me standing in the door of his home.

His house was the total opposite of Alderic's. The log cabin had large windows that allowed the sunlight to flood the space. Vines stretched the length of the wall, and a collection of simple herbs and plants filled the space. A worn leather couch set in front of a large television. And to the far left was a small kitchen. To the right, where Rhys was headed, was a den which he turned into a craft space.

"You really meant to make something, like with your hands." I lifted a tool from his workbench after following him inside. "So, you're crafty as well as skilled in witchcraft?"

"I guess you could say that." Rhys smiled and held his hand out to me. "Would you give me your stone please?"

"What?" I stepped back from his workbench; face flushed with heat.

The only stone I knew of was the one I nearly died to get. I'd been keeping it secure in my pocket since I had arrived there. I couldn't just hand it over to him. Rhys was nice and all, but after all I'd gone through to get it, I couldn't just give it away.

"Trust me, please?" He held his hand out to me. "I promise to give it back before you leave."

"You don't plan on keeping me here for the rest of my life, do you?" I stalled.

He laughed and shook his head no. Reluctantly, I did as he asked. The moment the stone left my hand, my heart tightened in my chest and my stomach twisted into knots.

He moved to a workbench next to a small window. Strips of wire, metal, and an assortment of random tools littered the surface. His back to me, I couldn't see what he was doing, so I moved to get a better view.

"What are you doing?" I peered around his shoulder.

"I figured I could make this a little easier for you to keep safe. Having it stuffed in your pocket isn't exactly failproof." He picked up a long wire and a small blowtorch. "Step back a bit, please?"

The torch lit up, and I watched him as he worked quickly, delicately wrapping the hot wire and molding it to fit the stone. He chewed his lip a bit and beads of sweat formed behind the safety goggles. I watched patiently, not wanting to distract him. When he finished, he dropped the piece into a bucket of water to allow it to cool.

"Where did you learn to do that?" I watched the steam rising from the water.

"My mother, she makes all types of sculptures and moldings for people." He took the goggles off and wiped the sweat from his forehead. "I picked it up pretty quickly as a kid."

"That is really impressive."

Using the tongs, he lifted the piece from the water and laid it out so that I could see it. "The loop here is so that you can put it on your chain and not have to worry about checking your pocket every five minutes to make sure you haven't lost it."

"This is really awesome of you." I examined how he wrapped the wire around in an intricate design. My stone set behind a tree and framed in the twisted wire. "This is so beautiful. Thank you so much."

"Of course." He smiled. "It's no problem. Are you hungry?"

"Yes, I could eat." I smiled and as if on cue, the deep gurgle sounded from my stomach and we both laughed.

"Good. I'll whip us up something." He looked at the chain around my neck again before we headed off to prepare lunch.

Rhys was also skilled in the kitchen. The meal he made was fresh and healthy, grilled salmon and spinach salad, which I devoured. He laughed at me and made jokes about how the myths were true about sirens and their love for seafood. My response was a laugh around a mouthful of food.

After lunch was over, we moved back to the basement, to my new favorite spot.

"How much more of this am I expected to go through?" I spoke to Rhys in hushed tones inside the room I'd dubbed the Serenity room. "I love this. Learning to control my power is great, but this is too much. And working with Alderic honestly makes me second guess myself more than anything. It barely even feels like I'm his daughter.

"I mean, when I block an attack or manage to get one in on him, he looks so proud. But when he told me all the stuff he wanted to teach me, I thought it would be fun. Instead, it feels like he is trying to turn me into a damn soldier. I feel stronger, yes, but I didn't know about all this, yet he acts like I should be a natural overnight. Yesterday's session ended with a bloody nose for me. All he did was smirk and hand me a towel."

"You're doing fine, Syrinada." Rhys took to rubbing my shoulders as the norm whenever we met in the Serenity room. Usually, Alderic was too busy running away to deal with something that was apparently urgent and much more important.

"Yes, but to be honest, if it weren't for you, I would have been on the lookout for the exit a long time ago." I moaned softly as he moved to my hand to continue the massage, moving from the tips of my fingers up my arm and back to my shoulders.

"He's too intense. I mean, I know there is so much I need to learn, but this just feels wrong. I feel like he is pushing too hard. Have you ever gotten a feeling in your gut that someone isn't telling you something? That's how I feel now, and I don't like it. I have spent too much of my life being lied to."

"You should try talking to him. Express how you feel. If he doesn't know, there is no way he'll ever change the way he's working with you. He was the same way with me when I first got here. All business. I'm sure he just doesn't realize the way it makes you feel."

"Sure, I could try talking to him, but when exactly am I supposed to do that? I mean, when he isn't yelling out commands and acting like a drill sergeant, he's locked away in his room like a hermit. We haven't spent more than a few minutes a day getting to know each other, which was his reasoning for me coming here. I don't know what I expected from this, or if I expected anything at all, but this isn't it."

I moved away from his touch to stretch and keep my thoughts on the right track. If he kept massaging me, soon I'd be too relaxed to get my point across. I played with the chain that hung around my neck that held the locket that Alderic had given me and now, right next to it, was my siren stone.

"I'm sorry. I don't know what to say. To be honest, I thought he'd be different once you were here." Rhys admitted and cracked his knuckles. "There have been some changes, you know. He doesn't mope around nearly as much as he did before. Still, I really thought that he would take the time to enjoy you more."

"Enjoy me?" I raised a brow.

"Yes, enjoy you," he winked. "Like how I do."

"You enjoy me?" I sat up and turned so I could see his face. Whatever he was about to say, I wanted to give him my full attention.

"I do. I enjoy your smile, and I look forward to your laughter. Everything you share with me is a gift that I cherish. Any moment that I've been able to spend here with you has fulfilled me in a way that I hadn't thought possible. You're this amazingly unexpected gift that when I think of the day when you are no longer here, causes my heart to ache."

He paused as he considered whether to continue his thought. It was a relief when he continued. I wanted to hear more.

"It may be odd to say this to you, and you can definitely tell me if it is, but I feel on some level, that you belong in my life. For the past few years, there has been this emptiness that I used to think was there because of my father's absence. I thought being here with Alderic had drummed up something deeper from my childhood, but I know now that I was wrong."

"Rhys," I took a deep breath.

How was I supposed to respond to something like that? I could only think of Malachi and how he'd once said something nearly identical to me. Rhys' words made me feel heavy with guilt. When I looked into his eyes, I felt happiness. I was eager to learn more about him and to forge a deeper connection.

That's what was missing with Malachi. That excitement, that deeper yearning. I wanted it to be there, but it never was. With Rhys, though our relationship remained an innocent one, I felt thrilled and energized by his presence. I wanted more of him.

"Yes?" He prompted me to say more. He wanted me to jump at the chance to agree with him and solidify what he confessed.

"How do you know it's not my siren side making you feel this way? It's a part of the package." It hurt to say the words aloud and to express my genuine fear.

What if I could never find someone to love me for me, and not for the power that I held over them? What if, without the allure of my melodic call, no one would ever genuinely want me? How could I ever be sure again that someone could look past the supernatural side of myself?

"You do know that I can reject you, right? It's my choice to stay, and I choose not to walk away. I understand why it would worry you, but it's different with me." Rhys grabbed my hand. "The thing about having those who came before us mess up is that protocols get put in place to prevent those mistakes from happening again.

"Thanks to those 'forbidden' couples such as your mother and father, the covens now perform special blessings on children at birth. They pay special attention to the males. During the ritual, they cast what is basically a protection spell, meant to keep us from being susceptible to your particular charm.

"It was a foolish misconception of those witches, that we wouldn't still find love in forbidden territories even without a magical pull. There have still been cases of those lost souls finding each other against all odds." He shrugged.

"Really, so if I were to sing my siren song, nothing would happen to you?" Call me a skeptic, but I needed more proof.

"It would be beautiful, and heart touching, I'm sure, but it would not leave me under your spell. If you want to, you can try it. Lay one on me now."

"Okay, if you're sure, I think I would like to try. I just have to know for sure." He nodded, and I stood up and distanced myself from him. He remained on the couch and watched me as I prepared myself.

I relaxed my body, emptied my mind, and allowed the call of my siren to rise from within me. As usual, my ears were deaf to the full effect of the song that came, but I could see its beauty in his expression. Relief came as I recognized it was still Rhys looking at me. He didn't look entranced like the others; he wasn't a zombie. He was present in his enjoyment.

My song continued, as my heart filled with happiness that I could share something so intimate with him. The deep rise and fall of his chest, the roll of his head as the symphony of sounds moved over him; he was enjoying it. He smiled at me. To further prove his point, and to put my mind at ease, as the melody continued, he stood from the couch and turned his back to me. With the same ease as when he first walked into my world, Rhys walked away.

When I stopped singing, I felt something I hadn't expected a swelling in my chest born of happiness and of... love. This man was the only man, human, siren, or not, that could love me for me and not for the power that I held over him. Even a merman, though they had ways of overpowering the siren's call, was still at a disadvantage. I knew that from personal experience.

Malachi and Demetrius both claimed to be immune to my persuasions, but the way they treated each other made me believe otherwise. They turned on one each other and sought to claim me as their own in an unnerving way. To think of them brought back an old feeling. Guilt. I'd not only broken the brothers; I'd left Malachi with no clue of where I was or if I was okay.

Rhys was right. As hard as it would be, I had to speak with my father. It was time for me to go back to Deuterio.

CHAPTER 18

I'm not sure how long I stood outside of Alderic's bedroom. His doors were closed, as always. It wasn't until I got there that I thought about how I'd never seen the inside of his room. In fact, I'd avoided it. Alderic obviously wanted it that way. As much as Alderic claimed to want to build a relationship, I could tell he was a private person. I tried to respect that.

Unfortunately, I'd searched the entire house looking for him and couldn't find him. This was my last resort. The conversation needed to happen before I lost all nerve to speak to him. I took a deep breath and a gulp of courage before my hand lifted to the door. I knocked three times and waited. There was no response. Another deep breath and then I repeated the effort. Again, there was nothing.

If only the daring side of me had stopped at knocking on the door. I tested the doorknob and found it unlocked. I could have turned away then, but I turned the handle and pushed the door open.

The ominous creak should have been enough to send me the other way, but again I was too brave for my own good. Inside, it was completely dark. His room was a sharp contrast to mine. He painted the walls the darkest shade of black and thick black drapes covered the windows, allowing no light from outside.

Basic magic came easily to me after my training, and I was able to illuminate the room by conjuring a small flame on the tip of my finger. With what it revealed to me, I wished like hell that I had just waited for Alderic to find me so that we could have our talk.

I could have left a note taped to the door, but it was far too late for that idea. My stomach turned because I couldn't erase what I saw from my mind. It wasn't as if I could just leave and pretend like I didn't see it, either. The need to know more would undoubtedly eat at me until it drove me insane.

I didn't recognize her at first, frozen as she was. I don't think I wanted to. She hung, suspended inside of a liquid tube, a relic. However, the features of her face and the resemblance to my own were undeniable. She had the same cheekbones, same slant of the lips, and even the same hair hung past her shoulders, highlighted in natural tones of red.

She was my mother. I lifted my hand to the moist barrier that surrounded her and examined her closer. How was she here? How was this even possible? It was really her. She was so close to me. I just wanted to feel her.

"Mom?" I whispered, and my pain turned to anger.

Hand still pressed against the cool barrier, a jolt of power flowed from my palm and into the fluid. It created a ripple on the surface. The barrier then hardened, shifting into glass and then it fractured. I lifted my hand, afraid that it would shatter.

When the sound of the glass cracking resonated through the room, I could have sworn I saw her move, as if she flinched from the sound, but that couldn't be right. She was dead and my father had frozen her in some romantic, yet creepy water coffin.

I wanted to stand there and stare at her forever. Even in silence, in that deafening moment when there was no possible exchange between the two of us, I felt at peace just to be near her. Before that shock, my heart felt healed in a way like it had never been before. My wish, as childish and naively optimistic as it sounded, was that the barrier between us would break and, through some strange magic, it would return her to me, alive.

Unfortunately, the reality of my situation settled in. If anything at all needed to happen, it was my erasing all evidence of my presence. Hell, if I could figure out how to reverse what I had done completely, that would have been the ultimate blessing. Alderic was one powerful and often ill-tempered man, and the last thing I needed was for him to turn that anger on me.

Something told me that our father-daughter relationship wasn't nearly as precious or strong enough for him to overlook my possibly destroying the one thing in the world he really held true to his heart.

The fire conjured at my fingertips gave enough light to see the work desk in the corner. It was littered with papers and seemed to be the best place to look for aid. Reluctantly, I left my mother to investigate the materials.

I shifted through the mess, often looking over my shoulder at her. The crack hadn't spread. That was a relief, but I still had to fix it.

Instead of spells, scribbles of magic, and potions, there were battle plans. Alderic had mapped out strategic moves in extreme and intricate detail. When I lifted the first layer of pages, I found sketches and spells, all of which were wrapped around my name.

Over and over, my name intertwined with a spell that repeat-ed, in different languages, the word 'sacrifice'. I read further and the pieces of the puzzle fit into place. My father, this man who claimed to have wanted me in his life to make up for lost time, only truly desired to use me as a sacrificial bomb against the covens.

"What are you doing in here?" Alderic's voice boomed be-hind me, and I froze.

I kept my eyes on the paper. He may have tried to work his magic on me if I turned to look at him. The same magic that lulled me into coming home with him. The anger, the betrayal, the emotions I felt were necessary to keep me focused on what really mattered. If I stayed focused, he wouldn't be able to sway me.

"What is this?" Back to him, I held up the papers which outlined his devious plot. All concern for his anger about what I had done left. He'd been lying to me from the moment I met him, plotting to use me as a damn weapon.

"You don't belong in here!" He went to my mother's body and examined the damages. "What have you done?!"

"I didn't mean to. I was trying to fix it." I finally turned to him. "I was looking for a spell or something to help me reverse it, but then I found all of this. What the hell is this? You didn't want me here because I'm your daughter and you love me. You brought me here so that you can turn me into a damn weapon!"

"It's okay, she is okay, and what are you doing in here?" It was as if nothing I said had registered with him. This man didn't care about me.

"I came to talk to you. I needed to talk to you." His eyes were still locked on my mother. I moved for the door.

"You needed to talk to me about what?" Alderic turned to me. "What could be so important that you would invade my private space?"

"I want to leave. I don't want to be here anymore." That did it; I had his full attention just as I made it to the door.

"You cannot leave!" The gust of power slammed the door shut and the locks sounded.

"You said that I could go home whenever I wanted." I pulled at the door handle, but it wouldn't budge. "Open the door!"

"Home? What home do you have? This is your home. Here with me!" The sound of his voice boomed and shook the walls.

"Why do you want me to stay? So, you can train me more, or so you can become more of a tyrant? Maybe it's so you can use me against the witches!" I struggled with the door, then punched it when it still would not open. "You lied to me!"

"I am your father, and you will do as I say!" He approached me and I pressed my back against the door.

The angry look in his eye made my stomach knot up. I was trapped with this man who wasn't at all what I thought he was. There was no way out.

"I will not! I won't fight a war I want no part in; you will not make me your sacrifice." I stood my ground. There was no way I was going to let him turn me into a weapon.

"You disobedient little—" He lifted his hand and threw his energy at me, knocking me away from the door and into the wall and then my dear old dad charged me.

My shoulder jammed against the wall and the pain had me near tears, but there was no time to think about it. As I watched him come for me with anger and hatred in his eyes, I focused my thoughts. Just as he taught me, I drew the energy towards me and then, returning his aggression, I forced it in his direction.

He flew backwards and landed just at my mother's feet. I looked at her; I didn't want to leave her, having just found out she was there. She was a ghost of herself, a shrine for a love who refused to let her go. I had to get away.

Before I made it back to my feet, Alderic was on his. He shot another blow of energy at me which I proudly dodged. For a moment, I panicked, but instinct took over when I glanced at the watery tomb. Like fire spreading across my brain came a primal understanding of what I needed to do.

I opened my mouth, focused on my father and released a sound so powerful it caused the crack on my mother's barrier to spread. Alderic screamed and doubled over as he covered his ears trying to block out the shrill sound. It didn't work.

Thick droplets of blood fell from his nose and his eyes rolled into the back of his head before he hit the floor. This time it looked like he was down for the count, but I knew it wouldn't keep him down for long. Once again, I pulled the same force of energy to me and used the practice of moving the wind to break down the door. It took a few tries, but it finally gave under the pressure. I ran out into the hall, calling for Rhys.

"What is it? What's wrong?" He appeared seconds after his name passed my lips, and I slammed into his chest.

"Get me out of here!" I screamed as he tried to hold me still.

"What the hell happened?" He saw I was holding my shoulder and immediately was ready to defend me against whatever had caused my injury.

"It doesn't matter; just get me out of here." I looked behind us. "Now!"

Alderic hadn't yet appeared, but it wouldn't be long. We needed to put as much distance between him and us as possible.

"Okay, come on." Rhys wasted no more time with questions.

Stepping outside, I stopped and gasped. The rolling hills and meadows that had met me when I'd first arrived were gone. Rhys didn't seem to notice at all. The lands were desolate and reeked of death and despair.

"What the hell happened out here?" I frowned as the smell made me want to vomit.

"What do you mean?" He tugged on my arm, helping me down the stairs.

"It didn't look like this when I first got here; this was all green and flourishing. This place looks like...like hell." From within the house came noises; Alderic was up and coming after us.

"I don't know what you mean, but we need to keep moving. Just keep running okay, and don't let go of my hand." Rhys started running just as I heard my father yelling from inside the house.

"Hurry!" I ran alongside him as fast as I could.

My legs burned, but I couldn't let up even for a moment. The sound of the door blown from its hinges and landing on the ground below was the last I heard as we crossed through a threshold of light and landed under the sea.

CHAPTER 19

"*Are you okay?*" Rhys asked as he checked me over.

My body was still sore, but I was healing fast. The water helped to speed the process. Already, my shoulder had stopped hurting and the pain in my back had eased up.

"Yes," I smiled at him and then I noticed he was still with two legs, and I completely freaked out. "Wait, you can't be here, you'll die!" I grabbed his arm and swam for the surface.

"Syrinada, stop. Just look at me, I'm fine. Magic, remember? I won't grow such a magnificent tail such as your own, but I'll survive." I slowed my swimming and looked at him.

I calmed as I remembered what Malachi said about the witches who came to sea. Their own magic protected them. I relaxed but felt like we were actors in a horror film, I waited for the scene to change and for this man who looked perfectly fine to suddenly be unable to breathe as the water flooded his lungs. Thankfully, that didn't happen.

"Are you sure you're okay? We can leave. We can go somewhere else." I looked at the surface of the water. "You don't have to be here; it isn't safe for you."

"Syrinada, we can't leave. This is where you need to be right now, or that jump would have landed us somewhere else. I let your energy lead us and it brought us here. That means there is something important here." Rhys looked around. "Whatever it is, I think you need to handle it before we move on."

We. He said we. Rhys wouldn't be leaving my side, and to know that gave my heart an unexpected jolt. Just beneath where we floated in the water was the city I previously thought was the most enchanting place my eyes had ever seen. That was no longer the case. All the grandeur of Xylon had been erased, leaving behind what appeared to be the ruins of such a place.

It was hard to accept what I saw. How could this be true? The beautiful underwater city was now in shambles. Buildings had collapsed and homes evacuated. I hadn't thought it possible, but the structures looked as if they had been set aflame. But what type of fire could burn beneath the sea?

We swam through the underwater streets and hoped that we could find signs of life, but there were none. I tried to remain optimistic. Just because we had found no one, didn't mean they were all dead. They could have gotten out and made it to a haven somewhere unknown. The first person we saw was one who brought a wave of relief.

"Malachi?" I couldn't help myself. I swam to him and wrapped my arms around his neck nearly cutting off his air. "You're okay, thank god!"

"Sy, where have you been? We all thought—" He didn't finish his thought.

We both knew what the assumption naturally would have been after I didn't return. It didn't help that I had taken extra time away to be with Alderic.

"I was with my father." That familiar friend, guilt returned to me.

How selfish of me was it to have left him waiting all this time with no word, and no idea of what happened to me? Yes, the magic of Alderic's home helped to blind me. I wasn't aware of the tricks, my father played on me when I first arrived at his home. It was still no excuse for my negligence after I figured it out.

"Your father, why?" it hurt him, I could tell. He'd spent his life protecting me from the very man who I'd so easily walked away with.

"He came to me, and I felt like I needed to go with him. Unfortunately, I found out he only wanted to use me in some sick revenge plot, so I left." I kept my answer simple because to go into further detail would bring back the sting from my father's betrayal.

"He just let you go?" Malachi raised a brow. "Just like that?"

"No, not exactly. I had to escape. It took some help." I nodded my head to the man at my side.

"From who?" Malachi asked, as if he hadn't seen Rhys there at all.

This was going to be an issue, and from the looks of things, we didn't have time for it.

"Me, hi, I'm Rhys. Nice to meet you." Rhys smiled and extended his hand to Malachi as an offer of peace.

"Oh, hi." Malachi responded nonchalantly.

For a moment, it looked as though male ego would prevent my protector from being cordial, but it didn't. He shook Rhys' hand and smiled, but his jaw was tight set. A very unconvincing display. Malachi wasn't okay with Rhys being there.

"What happened here?" The question was necessary both to end the awkward exchanged between the two men and to gather much needed information.

"We've been under continuous attack. The witches who ambushed us after we left Tylia's place went back to their coven with confirmation of your existence. They thought you would be here, and they came to take you away. At first it was peaceful, but when they couldn't find you, they thought we were hiding you and saw fit to destroy everything in their path until we handed you over."

"Where are they now?" Rhys asked Malachi and placed a hand on my shoulder to calm me.

My anxiety was palpable in the surrounding water. How could I let that happen to these people? Even if the group wasn't my biggest fans, they didn't deserve what had been done to them and to their homes.

"I'm not sure, but I'm willing to bet that they haven't gone far. They've been taking shots at us for the last two days." Malachi looked to the border of the city and showed which direction the attacks had come from. "Luckily, there haven't been many casualties. We were able to evacuate people to neighboring cities. Some were not lucky enough to make it out, others lost their lives as they were traveling. There are a lot of hungry creatures out there and we normally wouldn't travel in such large numbers."

"We have to help." Rhys moved forward. "Anything I can do, just let me know."

"Yes, please tell us what we can do." My eyes took in everything but Malachi's expression. The disappointment I was sure was there would have been too much to witness, and I needed to keep my head together. Knowing that I had hurt this man yet again would destroy me.

"Some of that witchy magic may just come in handy right about now." The deep voice was wrapped in a smile. My heart fluttered; this was real.

"Demetrius?" I swam to him and wrapped my arms around him. I touched his face. "Are you really here?"

"Yeah, Syrinada, of course I am." He laughed. "You didn't think that I'd go down that easily, did you?"

"I just don't understand how you are here." I touched his face and smiled. "But I'm glad you are."

"We can discuss that later," Malachi spoke and gave Demetrius an odd look.

"That place, it tricked me a few times. Made me think you were there, alive, but you weren't." I smiled and wiped my eyes.

"Well, I'm here and I'm fighting to protect this place." Demetrius nodded. "I'm okay."

"Good, I'm glad you are." I smiled.

"Your stone, you got it?" Demetrius asked.

"Yeah, it's here." I pulled the stone up, which hung safely on the chain with the locket that held my mother's faded photo.

"Wait, I thought you were supposed to absorb it." Malachi moved forward and pushed his brother. "What happened? Is something wrong? Are you hurt?"

"Nothing's wrong. I'm fine, trust me. That's what happens for a normal siren, but as we all know, I'm not normal. The rules are different." I dropped the chain and then let the stone rest once again against my chest.

"I see." He inspected the wire that wrapped around the stone and secured it to the chain.

"Rhys made it for me, so that I wouldn't lose it." I smiled at my new friend, who nodded his head to me.

"Well, that was nice of him." Demetrius nodded to Rhys, and then pulled me to the side. "We need to talk."

"About what?" My gut told me what he wanted to discuss, but for once, I wanted that nagging feeling to be wrong. I'd made a vow to this man, and he would want me to live up to it.

"If you two would give us a minute?" he said to the guys who hovered nearby.

Hesitantly, Malachi and Rhys both moved away in opposite directions. There would be no fast friendship there, not that I ever expected there to be.

"You made a decision, didn't you?" he whispered close to my ear.

"I don't know what you mean." Play dumb, yes that was the tactic I chose. It wouldn't work, but it was worth it just for a few more seconds of stalling.

"Yes, you do. Look, I understand. You thought I was dead but I'm not. You should know that bond is not one that is easily broken." He looked over his shoulder to be sure we were alone. "You're mated to me now. I feel it, the change between us and I know you feel it too, even if you want to deny it now."

"Does Malachi know?" What more was there to say? He was right. I knew it from the moment I hugged him. The vow I made in the naiad's presence was being enforced.

"I haven't told him, but you should already know how intuitive my brother is. If he hasn't figured it out by now, he will."

"What am I supposed to do?" I looked around Demetrius at his brother, who was still staring at the boundary lines of the city.

"For now, I suggest we focus on protecting Xylon. That's what matters now. We'll deal with the rest later."

"Sounds simple enough." I agreed. It was the best option.

"Great!" Demetrius clapped his hands and called the two guys over. "We need to get back to strategizing." He turned to me. "I really hope that you learned some awesome witchy defense tricks while you were away. We are sure as hell going to need them."

"I will work with her more. We can come up with some things," Rhys announced, and Malachi scoffed and swam away. "So, he isn't a fan of mine, huh?"

"Don't mind my little brother. He just doesn't like to share his things. Selfish little bugger he is." A cool chuckle and the eldest Denali brother swam away.

"Thank you for this." I spoke to Rhys as we followed the brothers close enough not to lose them, but not close enough that we could hear their conversation or that they could hear ours.

"Of course." Rhys smiled at me.

I shook my head because that smile would be the thing to destroy me. I wondered if he knew the effect he had on me, and even more if I had the same effect on him.

"You don't have to put yourself through all of this." Giving him an out was the right thing to do. He didn't have to put his life on the line for me or anyone else.

"I know, but I have this thing about sticking by the sides of the people I care about when they need me." He grabbed my hand and clenched it in his as we swam on. Ahead of us, Demetrius glanced over his shoulder and frowned at our joined hands.

CHAPTER 20

P*reparing for battle* was intense, as it should be. Reports came in of movement along the borders, but there were no attacks. I trained intensely with Rhys, who showed me more of the offensive strikes that my father had taught me. He'd completely switched gears and the fun and easy trainer was much more serious.

We both agreed that, though he was delusional and deceptive, Alderic was an excellent trainer. I was much more skilled than I'd thought. The magic mixed with the power of the siren created something completely intoxicating. I wielded it with ease and wanted to continue. Each time he called for a break in the session, I would beg that we continue.

"You were never like this before; I can't imagine you actually enjoying training." He laughed at me as we ended another session together. There had been little time for sleep, but in the last few days, we'd gotten hours of training in.

"It's different here. With my tail intact, I feel so much more in tune with my power." I boasted. The energy of the water also added to the way I felt. The underwater current fed me and made me feel invincible.

"Your siren is thriving here. That's something you may not be able to fully tap into when you're on land," Malachi spoke and entered the room Rhys and I had claimed as our own space.

"I'll give you two some alone time." Rhys quickly left us but gave Malachi a meaningful look before he did.

"You never told me, is that your new boyfriend?" He questioned in a tone that irritated me.

"He is a boy; he is a friend, so if that's what you want to call him, sure." I rolled my eyes. "Is that what you came in here for?"

Malachi filled the past few days with snide comments and remarks. It was the last thing I'd expected him to do. Yes, I knew it would upset him, but he acted like a child who'd just lost his favorite toy. I was no one's property.

At dinner the night before, he literally pushed Rhys from his seat next to me. Demetrius intervened, but I was seconds away from handling him myself. It was time for someone to knock some sense into him.

Demetrius knew how to calm his little brother down and they both disappeared for the rest of the night, leaving Rhys and me alone. Rhys acted as if it didn't bother him, but I could tell that he was also nearing the breaking point. There was only so much a person could take.

"I'm sorry." He touched my arm apologetically. "I swear I only came here to check on you."

"Well then check on me, and don't ask me leading questions to get more information from me about something that is none of your business." I moved away from him. The effect that he once had on me had diminished. It may have been because of his attitude, or possibly that I just wasn't that into him anymore.

"None of my business." Malachi scoffed. "Are you kidding me?"

"No, I'm not." I stared him straight in the eye. "I don't have to tell you everything about me. You know, I have a right to keep things to myself."

"Sy, I have been by your side this entire time!" He looked hurt, completely shattered by my words. "You come back here with this new guy and offer no explanation as to who he is. On top of that, you're acting like you don't trust me anymore."

"Yes, you have been by my side and that means a lot to me, more than you could ever know, but that doesn't give you the right to come in here and quiz me on things that are not up for public opinion." I confronted him. "And you know that this has nothing to do with whether or not I trust you."

"So, I'm right, you're with this guy now." He looked angry, enough that I feared his demon would show its face, but he had his stone in place around his neck. "I know something is up, Sy. You can try to deny it, but when you're near me, it's different, not like it was before. You can't tell me that everything is the same as when you left. That fire that was between us, it's gone now!"

"I'm sorry." I shook my head and backed away from him. "You're right. Things are not the same, but I don't owe you an explanation for that."

"Fine." He turned to walk away from me. "Fuck me for asking."

"Malachi..." I wanted him to stay and talk. I wanted to get some type of closure for all that we had been through.

I followed him, but before I could reach him, the building shook. The walls tremored and the sound of explosions echoed through the halls.

"They're here!" Rhys returned to the room. It had been days since the last attack from the witches, but we'd known they hadn't gone far. We'd just been waiting for their return.

The three of us barely made it out of the building when it collapsed. They knew exactly where we were, and they were throwing heavy fire. Demetrius met us soon after we exited the destroyed building. He was covered in dirt and grime and had a superficial cut on his arm.

"We have men moving in on them from behind, but we need to keep them distracted if we want this to work." He glanced at me and continued talking. "Are you guys up for this? Syrinada, do you think you can handle yourself?"

"Yes, I got this," I replied. I was shaken but still confident with my abilities.

"Good, let's go." Malachi swam away from us. He said nothing else to me and refused to look my way.

"Wait," I called out, but he continued swimming.

"Whatever you two were working on, this is the time to put it to use." Demetrius nodded to Rhys before he swam away. He didn't address what had happened between his brother and me.

"Are you sure that you're ready for this?" Rhys questioned.

"As ready as I'll ever be." I smiled. "How hard could this be? We're only going up against a group of warrior witches." I smiled.

"Yeah, you got this, you're a natural." His cool wink made my stomach clench. What if something were to happen to him?

Just then, another explosion sounded overhead. Rubble fell, but the water slowed its fall, giving us time to get away. We navigated our way to open space; it wasn't safe to be so close to the buildings. The blasts were intended to bring everyone out of hiding, and they did just that.

"We have to fire back!" I yelled over the sound of another building being leveled. "There isn't much more of this place left for them to demolish."

"Follow me!" Rhys swam ahead and further out into the opening.

He worked his magic like a puppeteer. Pulling its strings so that his will was done. First, he hit the opposition with a powerful ball of air that brought their attention to him. Within moments, they began firing back with everything they had. Fire strikes, water spears, everything came raining down on him, but nothing touched him. He held his own, and the sight of him working was mesmerizing.

I crept forward, assessing the situation. In the distance, Malachi and Demetrius moved stealthily on their path. From a distance I could barely make out that both had shifted into their demonic forms. The sounds of fighting, explosions, and cries of pain were the cacophony that fed my mind. My attention snapped back to Rhys, who cried out as a fire spear broke his shield and hit him in the arm.

"Are you okay?" I rushed to his side and inspected his wounds.

"Yes, I'm fine." He smiled, but his expression quickly changed as the scene behind my head turned drastic. "Watch out!"

I turned to see the fire coming at us. His shield was down, which left us completely unprotected. I held my hand up and focused on my magic. This was not the time to forget my training. The magic moved in my veins, and I focused on the incoming weapons. A deep breath and a command of my power, and they froze.

The spear tipped in fire hung in the water in front of us. Again, I commanded my power to influence their path, turning them on the ones who had launched them. I felt the power stronger than I had before and I loved it. The water aided me, moving a strong current behind each spear, adding more force to its landing.

Another, a wall of fire came at us, and again I moved the water itself to protect us. Shifting underwater waves moved everything within and pushed the witches further back. After I was sure he would be okay without me, I left Rhys' side and moved closer to the opposition. I called Demetrius and Malachi, who quickly came to my side.

Even in their hellish forms, neither of them frightened me as they had before. I could feel the power that they both had. Just as I was stronger in my siren form, they were stronger as demons. The two were on my flanks as I zeroed in on the enemy. There were at least two dozen who remained, and they had now redirected their attention and efforts to me.

Every powerful attack launched was aimed directly at me. I repeated my efforts, sending their fire right back to them. Each time, more of them burned and suffocated beneath the product of their own magic.

I called to the brothers, my protectors, and in the middle of battle, they came to me. Malachi and Demetrius fed me their energy through touch. Their lips touched my cheeks, neck and chest, their hands traveled across my torso and cupped my breast. Their physical interaction gave me the fuel I needed to keep fighting as I used my magic to protect us.

My tail tingled as the magic of both of my bloodlines continued to build. I pushed us further up and away from the underwater homes of my people. This was the time. I moaned as Malachi took his touches further.

We floated higher above the offenders who continued to launch attacks, but not one harmed us. It was when I heard them yelling that I brought my focus from the arousing touches of the men who clung to me. It was time to end it all. I pushed the brothers away, centered myself, and drew the borrowed energy into one powerful force of magic that shot from within.

My hands wielded the magic of my father, and my tail catapulted the force of my mother's blood. The explosion ripped their defenses apart. Those who survived fled. With the job done, my body felt heavy and sank to the ocean floor, but Demetrius was there to catch me. He yelled something at his brother and then pulled me towards the surface.

"Did I do it?" I asked him as he carried away me from the carnage.

"Yes. Syrinada, you did it. You really did it." He smiled down at me and held me tighter as he swam. "Hold on, almost there."

CHAPTER 21

My body broke through the surface of the water, supported by the powerful arms that still held me safe. The sun warmed my flesh rapidly and the healing effects were already at work. I wasn't sure if it was the water, the sun, or the man who held me which refueled my body, but either way, I was thankful. I opened my eyes and stared at the sky. I'd done what I set out to do.

"There's a beach not far away. I'll take you there," Demetrius spoke as he used his tail to push us in the shore's direction. "You need to rest."

"Why are you doing this?" My tone was low, and my words were slurred as if I'd spent the night drinking in Wicker Park as

I had done so many times. It would have been nice if that were the case.

"What do you mean? You need to be out of the water for a bit. Your body is spent, and you aren't completely siren. That's the setback for us mixed breeds. You can actually drown if you aren't careful, Syrinada." He kept talking as the water pushed against my body.

"Well, that's good to know." There wasn't much more to say and even if there was, my brain was too tired to concoct the words.

Instead of trying to continue the conversation, I relaxed my body and allowed him to tow me to the shore. It wasn't long before Malachi and Rhys climbed their way out of the ocean and joined us. The three men watched over me, each with their own unique mask of concern. I smiled at them all, happy to know that they would all be there to protect me and closed my eyes.

When I woke, it was dark and the smell of fish cooking over a fire made my stomach sound off. I sat up first and took in the ocean's beauty at night. The moon danced across the waves and the stars reflected their light just as beautifully. I wanted to stay in that moment forever, but again, the grumbles from my stomach told me it was time to do more. I tried to stand from my position, but quickly fell back on my ass. My grunt and yelp when I hit the ground, alerted the men that I was awake.

"You need help." Rhys made it to me first and helped me get up to my feet. My knees felt weak, barely capable of holding me upright.

"I'll be okay." I held onto him for support. "I'm hungry. Just wanted to get some food."

"No, Syrinada, you need to recover. Your body took on a lot of damage. I'll get it for you. You need to..." Rhys spoke as he tried to make me comfortable on the sand.

"I know what she needs." Malachi appeared and instead of helping Rhys' efforts, he lifted me into his arms and turned to carry me away.

My eyes were locked on Rhys. I didn't want to leave him. I didn't want to be away from him, but I was too weak to protest what was happening and my stomach growled again. I just wanted something to eat.

"Malachi, stop." Demetrius called out.

"Excuse me?" Malachi swung me around as he faced his brother. The motion made my head spin momentarily before a piercing headache kicked in.

"You cannot do this Malachi." The older brother's voice was calm.

This time, my stomach lurched for a different reason. Demetrius was going to reveal our little secret to Malachi. If only the man didn't have me in his arms just as he was about to be told just how badly I had betrayed him. He'd throw my ass back into the ocean to drown for sure.

"And why not? She needs to heal. What else would you have me do right now?" His grip was tightening around me and I wanted to scream and ask for him to put me down, but I couldn't. Instead, I remained hanging in his arms in a quiet panic.

"She needs to heal, yes." Demetrius nodded. "But you're not the one to help her with that."

"Oh, and who do you think should help her? You?" Malachi laughed at his brother. "This is low, man, even for you!"

"Yes, actually I am the one and it doesn't matter how you feel about it." Demetrius was losing his patience with his brother.

"Why is that? Is it because you're still trying to take her from me? This is not the time, Demetrius." Malachi turned to walk away, but the next words spoken brought him to a complete stop.

"She is my mate. Syrinada is bonded to me. Her choice, when it was required of her, was me. It wasn't you, as much as you wanted it to be." Demetrius announced.

Malachi's grip tightened more with each word his brother spoke. So much that the pain inspired tears to fall from my eyes.

"You're delusional." Malachi looked down at me; his worry couldn't be masked.

I said nothing because there was nothing to be said. Malachi knew his brother told the truth; it wasn't something he would lie about. He'd already said he knew something was different between us. He just hadn't known exactly what it was. The mystery was over.

"No, you are, and if you weren't, you'd have been able to see it by now." Demetrius tried to grab me from his brother's arms, but Malachi kicked him in the chest, sending him backwards. Demetrius was quickly back up on his feet. "I do not want to fight you, Malachi. I know that this is difficult for you."

"There is no way she chose you!" He scoffed. "For you to use this moment to convince me of otherwise is pathetic."

"Malachi," Demetrius stepped forward and moved to try once again to claim my limp body from his brother.

Driven by his own anger, Malachi dropped me on the sand, rougher than I would have liked, and stood protectively in front of me. "You cannot have her!"

"I told you I don't want to fight you but this is something you need to accept." Demetrius said assertively.

"You'll have to fight me if you want to get anywhere near her." Malachi was the one to make the first strike.

He slammed his fist into his brother's jaw and from that moment, the two were a blended mass of arms and legs. My dizzied mind made it impossible to tell who did what, but the sound of the landing blows, cries of pain and grunts of anger were illustration enough. Twice they nearly hit or stepped on me, at which point Rhys moved in to protect me from them.

"Stop it!" I yelled out into the madness in front of me and had to repeat the request multiple times before they complied. When the two forms stilled, Demetrius held Malachi in a head-lock. "You cannot continue to fight over me. I refuse to be the one to tear you two apart. You nearly lost each other for good. By the grace of whatever god watches over us, you two are still together. That is what should matter to you, not who is or who isn't mated to me."

"Syrinada, you chose me." Demetrius let his brother go and stepped closer to me. I held my hand up to stop him.

"You were my choice, yes, but that was only because I thought I'd never see you again." The words were hard to say, but they needed to be heard by both Demetrius and Malachi.

I could see their hearts breaking for two entirely different reasons. Malachi felt betrayed, and rightfully so. We had spent so much time together. He was my friend, my lover, and my protector, yet I had chosen another. What was worse was that I didn't choose the other person because I wanted him. I chose him so that I wouldn't have to tie myself to Malachi.

Demetrius was hurting as well. Though before he told me he understood the motive behind my choice; I could see in his eyes that he had hoped it would turn into more. He anticipated our relationship growing into something more significant, but that wouldn't happen.

"I'm sorry." I shook my head slowly. "But I don't want to be bonded to anyone, not in that way. I love you, both of you, but I cannot be what you want me to be."

"Sy," Malachi spoke my name and brought tears to my eyes.

His heartache was my own. This was the moment we would part ways. Walking away from this man was not something I could have ever prepared for, and it was something that I'd hoped would never come to pass. My expectations for our relationship were never clear. It never seemed pertinent to think about how far this journey would take us, but I couldn't hold on to him anymore. I had to leave him behind.

"I am so sorry." Those were the only words that came to me, but they weren't enough. It would never be enough.

Rhys helped me from the ground and we stood there in silence for a moment, hearts breaking over and over, until he nudged my shoulder. I turned from the two and, with the help of my new companion, I walked away. Just a few feet away, he opened a portal and grabbed my hand. He would take me somewhere safe.

The desire to glance over my shoulder was unbearable. If I looked back at them, would it send the wrong message? What would that say to them? Would it give them a false hope of my intentions to return? I had none at that moment. What would it do to me? Would it make me go back on a decision that my gut told me was the right one?

Instead of turning back to take in one last sight of the two beautiful men who had spent their lives protecting me, I kept my head forward, walked through the portal, and left the Denali brothers behind on the sandy shores.

CHAPTER 22

"*How are you feeling?*" Rhys' voice had become my soothing alarm each morning. Just as days before, turning to my side, revealed him sitting on the edge of the bed with a small smile and a wink.

"Getting there." My face warmed as I eased myself into an upright position and grabbed the cup of tea from his extended hand. "Good morning."

"Good morning. I'm glad to see that you're doing better." He sipped from his own cup. "I went for a jog today, it's absolutely beautiful out. When do you plan to leave this room?" He moved straight into what had become his routine round of questioning.

"I'm not sure. I don't know what will happen if I go out there." I pulled the sheets closer to my body. "It's safe for me here. If I stay here in bed, I cannot harm anyone."

"I told you, you're in control. You have been this entire time or else there would be men beating down our door as we speak." He chuckled. "That isn't happening, is it? You'll be fine, Syrinada. Nothing bad is going to happen."

Once again, he gave me the warm smile that melted my insides. I never told him how much I loved the way he said my name. Most people shortened it, Rhys didn't. In his voice, it was a melody that I replayed whenever my thoughts darkened. If he knew that, he would always do it and I would be jelly in his hands.

"Yeah, but if I lost control for even a second, a swarm of those entranced men both young and old would come rushing. I already know how something like that can turn ugly. Then the people we're hiding from will know exactly where to find us." I raised my eyebrow. Checkmate.

"Look." he paused for a moment, gathering his thoughts. This conversation had played out each morning for nearly two weeks and each time he was on the losing side of the discussion. Perhaps he was searching for a new strategy.

"I know what you're going to say, but I'm not ready." I spoke before he could continue. "We both know that this is a bad idea until I feel like I can handle it."

"Okay, well, I made breakfast." He lowered his eyes in defeat. "I guess I'll deliver it here, bedside service as usual."

"Thank you, Rhys. I really appreciate everything you've done for me. I know it hasn't been easy on you." If not for the knowledge that my siren had no effect on him, I would have felt guilty about having Rhys take care of me. He had, however, expressed to me countless times that caring for me was what he wanted to be doing. I'd never asked him to stay by my side. That was his choice.

We were staying in a condo that he owned. One listed under a pseudonym. He said it was his hideaway, and we would be safe, thanks to the wards he had installed. Not only were the witches after me, but my father, who had been in hiding for ages, would surely reconsider that approach to his existence.

Alderic didn't know about Rhys' dwelling outside of his home, or so we both hoped. Even though his wards were in place, we still used additional cloaking spells. Something still told me that even that wouldn't be good enough. If there were people who wanted me bad enough, eventually they would find me.

We'd been there for nearly a month, and I'd taken over of the master bed while he claimed a pull out in the front room. There was a second room, but he had it set up as a working office and studio for his art. No, we hadn't been intimate, which made my healing a much slower process.

Rhys offered, but it wasn't the way I wanted to heal. What would happen if we did? If we crossed that line, there was no going back. Every time I became injured, I would feed from him. I couldn't risk hurting him. I also really cared for Rhys and wanted our first time, should we get to that point in our relationship, to be a thing of passion and desire, not necessity.

Once more, I couldn't go that far with him because my dreams still took me back to Malachi. Each night, the yearning grew, but it was a desire caused by my want for physical interaction, not love. My longing for Malachi changed frequently. In some moments, it would be pure lust, and in others, it was the way one friend misses another.

I didn't love Malachi. Not the way he wanted me to. I couldn't call on him though; without a doubt, he would put his feelings aside and come to me. It wasn't fair to Malachi, and for me to start something with Rhys while still harboring emotions for someone else would be unfair to him as well.

Rhys did all he could to care for me, and at times, more than he should have. He fed me and made sure I had everything I needed. He drew me baths and washed my hair for me in the beginning, when I was too sore to do it myself. The man even went shopping and brought me clothing and other personal items. Anything I needed, all I had to do was ask, and sometimes even that was unnecessary.

We spent hours talking about nothing at all when sleep eluded me, and hours of silence, contemplating things we could not speak aloud. I wanted to spend more time with him. It felt normal. Not once did he shift into a demon, and my siren song called no men to their potential deaths. For the first time in a long time, I felt normal, and I wanted that to last.

After breakfast, as was our routine, we practiced more magic. He worked healing spells on me and made me soup and teas that helped speed up my heeling. I worked on pulling energy from nature, things that I couldn't kill. Plants that he would bring filled the room, and slowly breathed life into me .

It took time to learn not to turn a vibrant plant into a withering mess, but I had mastered it, and each day I pulled from them without harming. I also pulled from the sunlight that flooded the room and from the water that I took my baths in. This way of healing felt much more satisfying and left me with far less guilt on my conscious.

"Please come with me?" he asked again as he prepared to head to the farmer's market.

I'd asked him to look for more bamboo plants as they were my favorite and their energy gave me a buzz that differed from the other plants. He laughed at me and told me I was crazy but that he would look for some.

"Not today." I didn't feel up to this argument again.

"You need to get out." He sighed. "It's been too long of you hiding away in here."

"What I need is to continue resting." I responded this time with more edge to my voice.

"You aren't that bad off anymore. Now you are just milking it." He poked fun.

"Is that so?" I cocked my head. This was a new argument tactic for him. He'd never accused me of faking it before.

"Yep, I can tell by the way you wield your magic now. You're much stronger than you were even before the injuries." He pointed to the plants that lined the window. "Take the plants, for instance. I haven't been watering them at all and yet they flourish.

"That's because you haven't only been pulling energy from them, you've also been cycling it back. If you have energy enough to spare to keep these plants alive, and the control it takes to recycle your energy like that, then you're damn sure capable of taking a walk with me."

"Ah, I see." Using the campaign of the potential death of men came to mind, but he wouldn't let me pull that twice in one day and he hadn't ever brought the topic up more than once before.

"Yes, so no more excuses." he tossed clothing at me. "Get dressed, your highness. We're going for a walk."

"Okay, but if all hell breaks loose, I'm blaming you." I pointed my finger at him. He laughed and left me alone to get dressed.

The market was nothing special. A typical display. There were rows of booths, each with different offerings, which ranged from fresh fruits and vegetables to homemade soaps and honey. I stood next to a booth, sniffing a salve that reminded me of the concoction Verena crafted.

I wondered where she was. No one had seen her since she disappeared after our fight in the realm of the naiads. I'd expected to see her when I returned to the ocean, but assumed she had evacuated with the rest of the people. Malachi confirmed she had never returned.

"Have you found something you like?" The short girl on the other side of the table, whose name tag read Margaret, asked me. She was bagging up some soap for another customer, but kept her eyes locked intently on me.

"Yes, actually. How much for this salve?" I hadn't planned on purchasing anything outside of a new bamboo plant, but figured it would come in handy with my current track record.

With the way my life was going, there was no reasonable doubt that some magical trap wouldn't transport me back to that jungle. This time, I'd be prepared for running from the beast with no name.

"Do you have anything specific you need to care for? Perhaps I can recommend something more fitting for you." She smiled, and it spiked my paranoia.

Why was she looking at me as if she wanted to do more than sell me soaps? I couldn't tell what it was about the girl, but something was off and it made me want to distance myself from her.

"No, not really, but I've come to learn it's a good thing to have on hand," I responded nervously.

"That much is true. That'll be seven dollars." She smiled widely and looked around the table at other potential customers who were surveying her selection.

"Great, I'll take it." I handed her the cash and looked around, trying to spot Rhys in the crowd.

He'd been at the booth just across from my location looking at some potatoes that he thought would be good to cook for dinner. I swallowed the panic that rose in my throat when I didn't find him there. This was my first time out in the human realm after getting my stone. I didn't trust myself to be alone. Why would he leave me?

"Honey?" Margaret was holding out the small bag that held my salve.

"Um, thanks." I took it and walked out into the crowd.

I thought of calling out his name but didn't want to draw attention to myself. Neither of us had a cell phone, which, in hindsight, was a ridiculous thing to have done. Of course, we would get separated in such a large crowd. We should have made some sort of plan if we were split up. A meeting point where I could wait for him to find me.

My grip on the bag tightened as I plodded through the crowd, reminding myself to remain calm. He had to be near; he couldn't have gotten that far because I had only looked away from him for a moment. With each step, the panic slipped further.

The sun beating down on me didn't help the way I felt. My body already felt like it was quickly heating up. Sweat formed at my brow and my faced warmed with panic. I turned around, spinning in circles as I scanned the crowd, but still I couldn't spot him.

Moments later, I saw the face of the first man who looked at me with a type of hunger that led to trouble for a siren. He stopped everything he was doing, dropped his bags, and just stared at me. I moved past him, but I could tell he had turned to follow me. It kept happening. The further I went, the more men were affected. Totes of vegetables, handmade creams, and potted plants smashed to the ground and created a rolling sound of complete horror.

I quickened my pace, increasing my efforts to find Rhys increased. Women stopped. Some stared at me with complete hate, others with lust. This wasn't happening. I told him I wasn't ready. The moment I panicked, I'd lost what little control I had on myself.

I could hear the sounds of distress from behind me, but refused to turn around and find out the cause. I was sure it was because of me. All that mattered was finding Rhys and escaping.

Angry cries and sounds of fist landing on faces and other body parts finally prompted me to turn to see the mayhem behind me. The scene eliminated the option of remaining calm and locating my friend. Rhys was nowhere to be found and if I stayed there, things were going to get a lot worse. There had to be some way out, an exit, but all I could see were bodies. There were too many of them and they were all closing in on me. I was lost in a blur of bodies.

Hands touched and pulled at me. They were aggressive, tearing my shirt and pulling my hair from the pinned bun. These people would kill me if something didn't change soon. I had no choice. I had to protect myself. Overzealous, I unleashed a spell that I thought would create just a small pocket of space around me, one I could use to keep myself safe as I navigated through the crowd.

Instead, what I conjured was a force that sent bodies flying backwards. A ward of at least twenty feet pushed people into booths, knocked men into walls, and left one person unconscious. No one seemed to notice or care. They all just kept coming at me, hitting the barrier but no matter how much pain it caused, they just kept trying.

"Syrinada!" Finally, there was Rhys calling out to me. "Please, calm down."

"I can't. You said this wouldn't happen!" I yelled at him and cried. "You said I would be okay!"

"Look, we need to get out of here. You are in control and you have been this entire time. Just find that control again and we can go. Pull it all back into you." His voice held urgency, but he spoke with care.

"This is a disaster!" I screamed and continued to hold the entranced people at bay.

"Syrinada, please," his wide eyes were full of guilt. "Calm down."

"I told you I was not ready for this. I told you I shouldn't have come and now look. Look at them." I pointed to the fallen bodies. "They're hurting because of me."

"It will be okay." He was calm, sure, and he held my gaze.

I trusted him, and his eyes reminded me of that. I dropped the ward and walked to him as quickly as I could without bringing more attention to myself, but no one came for me. Instead, they stood around, pulling themselves up from the ground, each one with a look of confusion and disbelief.

"How can it be okay? Half of these people had their cell phones whipped out, recording that mess. We have to leave we can't stay here," I whispered as we walked away from the scene. He kept his arms around me as my hands still clutched the bag of salve.

"You don't have to worry about that." He held his arm around my shoulders. "We just need to get you home."

"Don't I? I mean, they will upload it to every media outlet in the world. Before long, the witches, the sirens, and every other entity that doesn't want me to exist will be on top of us." I still held the bag of salve in my hand and focused on that instead of the wreckage that we walked away from.

"The protection spell, it works against technology as well. None of those recordings will show anything. It will be as if a hundred cameras all suddenly malfunctioned at the same moment."

"Still, it isn't safe. I think we should leave." I kept my eyes on my hands and allowed Rhys to guide me.

"Okay, if you insist, we will. I have other safe houses we can go to." Still, his voice was calm, though he should have been furious with me for what I had done. How did I get so lucky to always have people like him, like Demetrius and Malachi, by my side?

"I'm so sorry for all of this." I stopped and looked up at him. Tears flooded my eyes.

"It isn't your fault." He lifted his finger to wipe away a tear that had fallen down my cheek. "We could have never seen that coming."

"I did." My guilt had returned in full force. I should have listened to my own instincts and not have allowed him to persuade me to leave. "Where were you?"

"I was right beside you the entire time."

"No, you weren't. I looked for you." I shook my head. "I called your name."

"Syrinada, I promise you I was right beside you. I answered you, I even touched your shoulder, but you couldn't see me."

"That doesn't make sense. Rhys, I looked for you. You weren't there."

"Fuck," he shook his head as if recognizing something. "Maybe you're right. We need to leave."

"So someone is messing with us?" I felt my face grow hot with anger. "Someone did that to me? Who could have done that?"

"Look, I'm going to make us something to eat, and you can take a bath. Relax. We can discuss it all later and go over our strategies. Right now we just need to get you home." Rhys placed his hand on my back ushering me forward. He looked back over his shoulder, paranoid that someone was following us.

CHAPTER 23

"*That smells amazing!*" I called out from the bedroom. Just dressed, after having enjoyed a much needed bath, the aroma of the meal Rhys had cooked filled the air and caused grumbles of hunger to sound from my stomach.

"Glad you think so." He entered with a smile on his face. "It'll be ready soon."

"I can't wait." I nodded.

"Are you feeling better?" He paused by the door.

"Yes, still a little shaken, but I'm okay now." My time in the bath gave me the space to think through what happened. I couldn't be angry at him and I had to be easier on myself. Despite everything that I'd been through in the past months, I was still new to the life of being a siren. I had a lot to learn.

"I'm glad you're feeling better." Rhys crossed the room carefully, arms opened to me.

I accepted the invitation and allowed his arms to wrap around my body. The embrace warmed my heart, and I relaxed into him.

"This is nice." I smiled against his chest and couldn't help but compare him to Malachi.

When I messed up around Malachi, he scolded me and made me feel like I was the worst person. Rhys didn't do that. He was calm, understanding, and forgiving. That was what I needed in my life. If I could have remained in his arms forever, I would have. Unfortunately, the oven timer rang out, interrupting my moment of comfort.

"I need to get that." He sighed.

"Yes, please. I don't want burned potatoes for dinner." I winked as he released his hold on me and walked out of the room.

I sat on the bed and looked at the plants and I felt full. Even in the chaos, Rhys remembered the bamboo plant. There was so much we needed to discuss our next move, and I couldn't help but wonder what our options were. Did he have another hideaway we could go to? Was there a spell strong enough to keep us safe? A loud banging noise interrupted my contemplation.

At first, it seemed as if the ruckus was caused by a neighbor, but then it came again and it was unmistakable that the bang was targeted. The walls shook with another boom as I ran out of the room to find Rhys, who'd come from the kitchen in search of his own answers.

"What the hell was that?" I asked.

Before he could answer my question, the door flew open and slammed against the wall. The impact was so strong that the hinges barely held it in place. Balls of light exploded into the room and blinded us both. My arms shielded my face but did little to lessen the confusion the flash of light caused.

"Rhys?" I called out to him but dared not to move. Instead, I dropped to my knees to make myself less of a target for our attacker.

"I'm here, my leg is fucked though." The sound of his voice was the anchor needed to pull us closer together.

My only thought was that if I could get to him, I could heal him. Before I made it to him, a hand fisted into my hair, pulled me back, and dragged me along the floor. I grabbed the arm that held me and tried to free myself but failed.

"Let me go!" I yelled just before they tossed my body against the wall.

Contrary to what I would have believed, it was a small woman who stood in front of me. She had the innocent look of a doll, but everything else about her appearance proved that this was not the case. Leather clad from head to toe, with a pair of thigh-high leather combat boots to match. She stared at me with an expressionless mask as she rolled flames across her fingertips.

"After what I saw today, you know I should just kill you now. Unfortunately for me, those are not my orders and I happen to be a good little soldier." She tilted her head to the side with a slight smile. "My instructions, however did not say that I couldn't have a little fun with you first."

"Who sent you?" My hand was at the back of my head. The bitch had actually taken out some of my hair!

"The covens, of course. You didn't think that you could get far without them finding you, did you? I should hope not, especially if your plan is to go on creating the havoc you did today." She squatted in front of me.

"They took five men to the hospital after you left, one with severely broken bones. Of course, they have no explanations for any of it, though I am sure the cleanup crews will make sure that all inquiries go away."

"What cleanup crew?" All I could think of was to stall her until I came up with a plan to elude the small woman. My body, however, was not on board with my brain. My legs were heavy and a dull pain rolled through me.

"Yeah. See, there are guys who show up when people like you step out of line and nearly expose an entire hidden world of supernatural beings. Don't beat yourself up; you aren't the only moron around."

"It was an accident," I groaned as the pain through my body set in. There was no way I should be in such pain. She had to have done something to me.

"Yeah, I'm sure it was. You okay, hun?" She smiled at me, knowing that she'd worked some type of magic to keep me sedated.

"Who are you?" I needed more time to fight through it. Deep breaths pulled the life of nearby plants to me and I could feel her spell wearing off. I just had to keep her busy, keep her talking.

"If you must know, though I am not sure why, my name is Maggie. It is so very nice to meet you, Syrinada. I've heard a lot about you," she said it as if she was actually happy to meet me; this woman was clearly psychotic.

"Maggie? You're the woman from the farmers' market." I recognized her then. Her wardrobe changed from the first time I saw her. Less innocence, more death dealer. "You did all of this, didn't you?"

"Maybe I did and maybe I didn't." It was true; this was the same person who sold me the salve. Only then, she looked so plain yet our interaction felt creepy, and now I knew why.

"How could you put those people at risk like that?" The witches were supposed to be so concerned with life continuing, but time and time again, I witnessed them at the core of catastrophe. What gave them the right to pass judgment when they were so clearly flawed?

"You know, the rumor is that you recently got your siren stone, which makes you an even bigger threat to our people." Flames still danced across her fingertips as she spoke. She wanted me to fear her. "As if you being a hybrid weren't enough to worry about.

"Your father's power; the lineage of his family is strong, and would you look at that, we can say the same about your mother! So, of course, no one wants to allow such an abomination to exist. You had to be tested, so I issued the test, and you failed."

"You're here to kill me?" I scoffed. "I already passed the naiad's test. How is this fair?"

"Oh, open your ears, woman. No, I am not here to kill you. I am here to collect you, and take you back to the covens so that the high council can determine what is to be done with you. Just call me your cabbie, Maggie!" Her hand threw the flames from her fingertips in my direction. I tried to move, but the projectile slammed into my arm.

I went on the offensive and threw my own brand of magic at her. The same force I used at the market, I pushed towards her. She fell back sliding across the hardwood floor until her back his the wall.

Maggie looked up at me, wiping the blood from her lip. "Now, that's what I'm talking about."

"You're insane." I said as I struggled to get to my feet.

"Yeah, maybe." She called the flames back to her hand and threw another blast at me.

This time I jumped out of the way, landing against the couch as I pushed another wall of energy at her, making contact for the second time.

Hit after hit, we dodged one another's attacks and destroyed Rhys' apartment while we fought. It was when we both threw our forces out and they collided between us that the world went blank. Blinded and hurting, I fell over a small chair and landed on my back. The piercing noise, the result of the explosion, was all that I could hear.

Before I could stand, the ringing in my ears needed to stop. I clamped my hands over my ears, but it didn't stop. When I tried to stand, I fell back to the floor. The piercing noise made me cringe, and no longer felt like an external assault. It was inside my mind, like nails across a chalkboard.

I took deep breaths, hoping for relief to come. I couldn't leave myself defenseless for too long. Maggie could attack again. I reached for the chair I tripped over, but it wasn't there. I wanted to call out to Rhys, but I realized that something heavy hung around my neck.

I lifted my hand to find myself chained like a dog. When did she do it?

"You bitch," I called out as the ringing in my head finally eased and the space around me came into focus. "Where the hell am I?"

I was no longer inside the condo that sat high above the busy city. She chained me to a wall in a dirty room with cement floors and a heavy metal door. Little light afforded me an obstructed view of the space.

Pulling at the restraint was useless. The spell she used to weaken me was still working and the plants that were aiding my recovery were now far away. The wall behind me served as a brace as the wave of vertigo passed over me and the sound of women talking replaced the internal shrieking against my eardrums.

They weren't in the same room as me, but they were close enough that I could hear my name as it crossed their lips several times. They spoke about me as if I was a plague to be taken out. The hatred in some of their tones turned my stomach, but the softness in others gave me hope. Regardless of what side would win the nearby debate, my only concern was to find some way to escape.

The scent of jasmine but blended with a powerful stench that stung my nostrils wafted through the room. Whenever I thought I was used to the smell, it would come back on me stronger. Each new flooding of fragrance came with less of the sweet aroma of the jasmine. The stronger scent caused my eyes to water.

The heat in the room rose every few minutes. My body temperature elevated until my face felt flush and my clothes clung to my body, heavy with moisture. Sweat poured from my brow, the salty drops stung my eyes, and the room became warmer as time passed.

"Girl," an old woman approached me.

She was tall and frail. Her body as thin as the bones her skin covered, but her presence was a strong one. She had skin so dark she nearly blended in with the shadows of the room. Long straightened locks of gray, which were a beautiful contrast to her complexion, fell to her waist and framed her thin face.

"The time has come for your judgement." She announced with disgust.

"You already judged me." My voice was raspy, dry from the heat in the room. "I did your test, and I succeeded; I got my stone. Yet here I am, suffering as you choose. Why are you doing this to me?" I held the chain that hung from the collar around my neck up so that she could clearly see it.

"You are an abomination to our kind." It was a statement of fact. This woman believed that I was exactly as she called me, an abomination.

"If that's the case, why not just kill me?" I countered. "Why bring me here to torture and toy with me?"

"Never has it been my place to decide if someone deserves to live. But I do know that what lives in you is evil. What else could it be when it is the product of lies and mistrust?" She scrutinized my face and body with her eyes and frowned. "How to handle that is something the spirits will tell us."

"Excuse me?" I'd heard of the spirits the witches used to aid their hand.

Not all magic was naturally born. Some had to be borrowed from the things that surrounded us, like the earth and air. In extreme cases, the most powerful witches could call on spirits from the other side. Witches who had died and taken their magic with them to the afterlife.

"The ancestors, they are here now, observing you. They will decide." She rolled her eyes as if offended I hadn't known exactly what she was speaking of.

Why the hell would I know about her procedures if never taught? The basic knowledge that I had was only recently made available to me. Maybe if I wasn't so busy running for my life, I could have taken up a class or two.

"I don't care what your ancestors think of me. What gives them the right to judge me? I didn't ask for this. I haven't hurt anyone!"

"You will watch your mouth, girl! They're your ancestors as well. It is our blood that runs through your veins just as it is that of the sirens. That same blood connects you to them and this coven! You will show respect. Do not sit here and spit your lies." She pushed a cup that I hadn't realized she was holding into my face.

I shook my head no; I wouldn't drink from her. For all I knew, she was trying to poison me. Hell, with the way she looked at me, odds were, she had every intent to kill me.

"Lies? What lies have I told?" I moved back to put distance between us, and the old lady's expression twisted into a scowl.

"You say that you have harmed no one? What about the men you sucked dry and burned to ashes? What about the sirens who now live without a home? Have you also forgotten about the brothers you have destroyed? Yes, they are your sort, but still you've hurt them. Their pain lies on your head."

"Those men hurt me first. They attacked me!" I defended my actions. "You call yourself judging me, but those sirens are without homes, thanks to you and your people. How can you blame me for that?"

I couldn't really deny the brothers. I had hurt them, not intentionally, but it was me who caused the rift in their relationship. If not for me, they would have never turned on each other. Still, I didn't ask for them to want me. I never wanted to mate with either of them.

"We did what we had to do. In your case, you could have left well enough alone." She pointed her frail finger in my face. "You got away from those men who hurt you. You were free of them, yet you went back to find them."

"You think I should have just let them be? I should have let them roam the earth aiming to hurt more women like they hurt me?" I shook my head no. "Besides, I couldn't control myself!"

"All of it was your choice. Now is not the time to play the victim!" Again, she shoved the cup into my face, and I moved away from it.

"What do you want from me? I didn't know I could do those things. You say that you have been watching me. You should know that much about me. They kept all this secret. Yet you expect for me to have some divine knowledge about things I once would have never thought possible." I wanted to keep standing, walk away from the woman, but I couldn't. Maggie's spell was only getting stronger, and my body grew weaker.

"Yes, we know all about your aunt's deceit. But when you figured out that you could learn to control yourself, you continued your misguided actions even with your friend's attempts to warn you of what the consequences would be. You allowed that darkness to overtake you. If it could push you so far to take another person's life, there is no telling how much damage you would do if left out in the world."

"This is not fair." Yes, I made mistakes, but everyone does.

How could she possibly stand there and judge me as if her life was squeaky clean and lived by the book? Everyone strayed. I couldn't think of one person I knew who hadn't made a wrong choice in their life. To top it off, she wasn't just judging me based on my past. No that would make sense. She made determinations about me based on a future that she determined plausible. She was judging me on crimes I hadn't even committed.

"Who said that it should be?" The old woman shook her head, causing her hair to sway and release more of the pungent smell. It was her, the scent that caused my head to spin and eyes to tear. "Drink the tea."

"I don't want your tea." I waved my hand at her and tried to push the cup from my face.

"It doesn't matter if you want it or not, you will drink it." She snapped her fingers, and two stocky young women came into the room.

They grabbed my arms and shoulders and held me in place as the old woman opened my mouth and poured the hot drink down my throat. I choked on the taste and tried to spit it out, but she slapped her hand over my mouth and pinched my nose, forcing me to swallow it.

It didn't take long before the drink settled in my belly and boiled my insides. The women hadn't even made it out of the room when I clutched my stomach, hunched over, and threw up everything by my stomach itself.

CHAPTER 24

Hours passed as I sat in that room and smelled the powerful odor of incense and burning herbs. I vomited until I had nothing left to give and after that, I still heaved as if still trying to expel something that wasn't there.

After that, what I thought were hallucinations began. My stomach burned, sweat covered every inch of my body, and my throat was raw. My vision doubled, and I lacked the energy to lift my body from the floor again. I sat there and waited to be judged and to be put out of my misery.

"Your spirit is strong young girl." A majestic voice interrupted my internal torture. The voice stood on a level all its own and reached deep into me to stroke my heart.

"Who's there?" My voice was a shaky comparison. My mind struggled with exhaustion, unsure of what to expect.

"My name is Amelia." The smile around the voice caused a small grin to stretch across my own face before I heaved again.

"Show yourself. Why are you hiding?" It reminded me of the naiad, her magical voice and beautiful appearance that all turned out to be a mask for the monster beneath. If Amelia was the same thing, I wanted to get the revelation over with quickly.

"I have nothing to hide." She appeared and was nothing like what anything I would expect from what was obviously a ghost.

She stood in front of me in solid form. A physical representation of beauty, accompanied by a glow of warmth that filled the room. Amelia had carob skin with a bald head and large gold earrings. Her eyes were enormous and the color of cognac. When she smiled, I felt my world pause.

"Who are you?" Intimidation turned my voice to a whisper.

"I am one of many, your ancestors. It is we who will decide." She looked at me with a mixture of sorrow and joy in her eyes. The puzzle of her emotions caused a tightness in my chest. What would she say, how would she judge me?

"You all want me dead. I can do nothing to stop you." I stared at her and wondered how a person who looked so loving could be possible of sentencing me to my death.

"Why do you not use your magic to escape this place? You are powerful enough, that much I can sense within you." She stood still, her arms behind her back.

A long gown flowed around her, though there was no air. The cream fabric had flakes of gold that danced in the candlelight and made the deep tones of her melanin rich skin stand out even more. She was gorgeous and powerful and it was at her will.

"What would be the point? Even if I make it out of here, you'll only continue to chase me. You will hurt my friends and my family; that much I already know. Look what happened to Xylon. The lives of others are of no consequence to you. They would destroy countless innocent lives to get to me. I can't sit by and watch that happen anymore. Do what you will with me."

"And you're okay with that?" She asked carefully.

"Look, I'm not going to sit here and lie and say that I think I deserve your hatred or punishment, if that is what you're asking. But after what just happened, the coven has made it perfectly clear that I have no say in what they want to do." I moved to sit against the wall. Having my back against the hard surface helped to stop the motion sickness I was experiencing, even though I hadn't moved an inch.

"You would let us take your life so easily?" She looked almost disappointed that I hadn't put up more of a fight.

"What would you do if you were in my place?" I looked into those large, warm eyes. "Tell me, what you would do if it were your life versus countless others. Everyone keeps telling me I'm a monster, an abomination and yet no one seems willing to give me the chance to prove them wrong. They marked me guilty at birth, no room to show otherwise. All of this is because of who my parents are, which is something I had no choice over.

"My friends and anyone else who dares to get close to me, anyone who loves me, are at risk. What would you have me do? I cannot be so selfish as to put my life above theirs when they have already risked so much just by helping me. So no, my answer is no.

"It is not a simple decision; it is not an easy choice. Easy would be to run, easy would be to use the power I feel stirring inside of me to fight off whatever spell that bitch put on me. You're right, I can feel it there, my power, and if I called to it, it would come.

"Easy would be to hide from you for an eternity. This, this choice to not have to live my life like that, is the most difficult one I have ever had to make." My voice cracked as the last words passed through my lips. It was all true, and it was devastating. Still, I held back the tears that threatened to flood my sight.

I thought she would continue her conversation with me, but she didn't. With no formalities, the woman vanished, and I was left alone. At least the vomiting and choking heaves had stopped. I could breathe again.

No one returned to me. Not the judgmental old witch, her two buff handlers, or the little one who had brought me there. What I told Amelia was the truth. I could still feel my power within me and as she said, if I wanted to, I could easily leave, even with Maggie's magical sedation.

I hadn't realized it until Amelia said it. My power was strong, yet for whatever reason, I ignored it. Even after she pointed it out to me, I sat weak against the wall and remained there. What I did was reach out to Rhys as he had taught me during my training.

It wasn't something my father wanted him to show me. Rhys made me promise Alderic would never know about that part of our lesson. He never said it, but that was the moment I suspected that my new friend didn't have as much trust in my father as he said he did. It was a simple process, really.

"Every person has his or her own unique frequency. Anyone you encounter, you unknowingly tap into that frequency, and it stays with you in the back of your mind. Through a special sort of meditation, if given the right circumstances, you can reach out to that person using telepathy." He explained to me.

The first time we successfully did it, I'd been in the fluffy bed covered in pink, and he used that moment to tell me how proud he was of me. My wish in that moment as I waited to be judged was that after all that we had been through; he was still just as proud.

"Rhys? Are you okay?" I spoke with my mind and waited for a response. I could feel him, and I knew he was on the other side.

"Syrinada, what happened? Where are you? Are you hurt? Tell me where you are and I will come to you." He rushed his thoughts, obviously afraid our connection wouldn't last.

"No, I can't tell you that. I'm fine. How is your leg? Please tell me you're okay." The tears I held onto threatened to break free. How could I say goodbye to him? That was the point of my call, after all.

"I'm fine. My leg will heal. What matters now is making sure that you're safe. Why can't you tell me where you are?"

"I'm so sorry that they hurt you."

"Listen to me, I am okay. Please tell me where you are so I can come get you."

"I can't do that. This is something I have to do on my own." I don't know how, but I knew that if Rhys showed up, it would be bad for him. "Please, just trust that I'm making the right decision."

"Syrinada, please don't make me sit by while they take you from me." I felt the pain in his thoughts, his heart breaking. "I can't bear to lose you."

"Rhys, please take care of yourself." I cut the communication then.

I couldn't take it anymore, hurting him as I had hurt so many others. The tears that fell across my cheeks reminded me that though it would be hard, I couldn't put anyone else's happiness beneath my own. Coming to save me would not end well for Rhys, even if he couldn't see that now. I couldn't allow him to stand against the coven.

"Why didn't you tell the young man where you were?"

I lifted my tear-stained face to see a man.

He was elderly with pale skin and snowy white hair. He stood proud. Wearing a three-piece suit fitted with a top hat and a pocket watch. I would have smiled at his appearance if I hadn't been in mourning for myself.

"I couldn't tell him. Couldn't risk him coming here." I wanted to ask this man's name, but something told me not to.

He didn't seem nearly as friendly or easy going as Amelia. He reminded me of the man from the naiads' walk. The witch who protected the gold, the two could have been brothers.

"Why not? He would have saved you." He nodded slowly. "The boy is powerful enough."

"It's not worth it. All of that for me. How many others would it hurt? I'm not just worried about Rhys, but the people who live here. Regardless of what they think of me, I'm not some horrible person. I don't want them to get hurt, and I know he would do whatever it takes to get to me. How could I live with myself knowing that I allowed that to happen? Rhys loves his people even if he doesn't always agree with their ways. I will not be the tool that rips him apart from that."

"Interesting," he said simply, and then he was gone. I never got his name, but he left me with the scent of embers. My gut told me that should I allow myself to become familiar with the spirit, whose smell would be with me forever.

I sat on the floor with my back against the wall. The smell of my own vomit caused me to feel ill again and this time accompanying the nausea were dizzy spells. I tried to distance myself from it as best as I could, but the heat of the room only amplified the odor.

I closed my eyes and thought of Malachi. Where was he? Was he okay? In that moment, I felt an extreme remorse for what I'd done to him and all the pain I had caused him. I hoped he and Demetrius could patch the holes in their relationship that were caused because of me. Still, even with that guiltiness, I knew I had done the right thing by walking away from them.

I could never remain bonded to Demetrius and as much as I cared for Malachi, he wasn't the one for me either. He'd always been there, yes, but proximity didn't equate to an eternal companion. Would he ever be able to forgive me? Maybe not, but I'd rather him hate me, and find true happiness than to have him spend his life chasing after a love and commitment that I could never give him. That would be truly selfish. To hold his heart and never intend to give him my own, I could never be so cruel.

The array of sounds that came from beyond the door interrupted my quiet introspection. The women had returned and were talking again. In a raucous debate, they voiced their speculations about how the spirits would judge me and wondered if they should come in and check on me.

The older woman who forced the rancid tea down my throat spoke. Her voice was unmistakable. She told them not to come near the door. She would know when it was time. If they interrupted the process, there would be consequences.

Apparently, summoning the spirits and not allowing them to complete the requested task without fail would mean a sacrifice of some sort would be needed to repent for the mistake. I wanted to know more, but they all shuffled further away from the door after that.

"He would take you back." This time, a small girl appeared. She wore a short white dress and her hair in braids that were pulled back to fall down her back. "My name is Ebon. Yes, I know I'm a child, but we have no control over when our mortal end comes. I was still one of three most powerful witches in my time. This, however, is not about me or my appearance, so you can stop staring like that."

"I'm sorry." I dropped my gaze from her face. The last thing I needed was to insult one who literally held my life in her hand.

"No need. It's not the first nor will it be the last time that my presence astonishes. I want to know about Malachi." She was the first to approach me without hesitation. She sat down in front of me with her legs crossed and leaned in close to me as if it would help her better hear my words.

"Why?" I wiped tears from my face pointlessly as fresh ones quickly replaced them.

"He is an important part of your journey. If you should make it out of here, you will cross paths with him again," she spoke it as a fact.

"Oh." The swell in my chest was undeniable. To know that Malachi was not entirely lost to me brought me happiness, which, of course, made me feel like shit.

"The world isn't as big as it seems and yes, he'll look for you. He already has been, in fact. When he finds you, he will forgive you, but he will also ask that you change your choice." She continued to get closer to my face, leaning in bit by bit. My body remained still, and tears still fell from my face. What was my response supposed to be?

"I can't." There was not a doubt in my mind. Malachi wasn't the one for me. How could he ever expect that of me after all that I had done?

"Are you sure of that?" She challenged me with the wide eyes of innocence. "It's easy to say what you will or won't do, but you never really know until you're in the situation."

"I can't hurt him like that." I shook my head, denying the claim.

"You would make him happy. How do you see that as hurting him?" She continued to pry and ask me what seemed like the same question, just in a different format each time.

"It would all be a lie. I am incapable of loving him in that way. At least I believe I am. I've tried. When he was hurting from losing his brother, I was there for him. I wanted so much for it to be more than my simply being there for a friend, but that was all it was. If in that moment, the lowest point of his life, I couldn't give him my heart, how can I ever?"

"How do you know this? Maybe you would change your mind." Again, the same question.

"The risk that I would not isn't one I think is worth taking. Malachi may not be happy with my choice but if we are meant to be in each other's lives, then it will happen and I won't have to lie to him to make it happen."

"What of the brother?" She eased back a bit, and I took it to mean that she was satisfied with my responses.

"Demetrius," I thought about the brother I was still bonded to.

How did I feel about him? Besides physical attraction, I hardly knew anything about the man. I knew that my feelings for him weren't nearly as strong as they were for his younger brother.

"There's nothing there. Besides, there is already someone else who loves him much more than I could ever." I nodded, thinking of Verena. "If he can ever see it, I know that's where he will find his true happiness."

"How can you know this?" Ebon asked. "I didn't know you possessed the gift of clairvoyance."

"I admit it is only my assumption, but I know Verena cares about him much more than I do. There was a moment once. I didn't see it at the time, but he looked at her, and something was there. When he saw her, his entire world lit up, and it was only for a moment, but it was there. They belong to each other. I hope that one day he realizes it."

"What about your father?" Again, with more questions, but this one threw me for a loop.

"Excuse me?" I stiffened. What could she possibly want to know about him? If she wanted inside information on how to find him, I wouldn't be able to give it to her. I didn't know how to get back to his house, not that I would ever willingly go back.

"Your father, he wants you by his side." She clarified.

"Yes, he does." I sighed and dropped my head back against the wall.

My mind and body felt broken and disconnected. Alderic was the last person I wanted to think about. He deceived me, and I still hadn't figured out what was going on with him or what he was doing with my mother's body.

"Will you join him?" The calm of the room disappeared and my stomach twisted into knots. This was the question that really mattered.

"No. All he wants to do is use me for his own selfish plot. I'm not even sure if he truly cares about me." It hurt to say, but it was true.

My father searched for years to find me just so that he could use me as a weapon against his enemy. He didn't love me as a daughter; he loved me as a tool for destruction. If that fight ended with my demise, he'd probably head back to the drawing board, eager to craft another way to seek his revenge. I doubted he would even mourn for me.

"He will come for you. You are smart enough to know this." Her smile was less genuine now.

Ebon pitied my life, the mess that it was, and I could do nothing but continue to cry. Not once had the tears stopped falling from my eyes and thoughts of my father only increased the flow down my face.

"Yeah, I get it. I will deal with that if, or should I say, when it happens."

"I think you're a smart girl, and you're strong. That will work in your favor." She stood, touched my forehead, and vanished.

Again, I was alone and there was nothing to distract me from my thoughts. Ebon had brought up so many valid concerns. The relationships in my life needed some real evaluation. Luckily, my foul smelling cell gave me nothing but time to think about them, or so I thought. The door to the room opened and the old woman reappeared.

"You're free to go," the woman announced, obviously not thrilled with the turn of events.

Disappointment written all over her face, she rolled her eyes. The old bag really wanted a different outcome, but luck was on my side, apparently.

"That's it?" I carefully stood from my seat on the floor and wiped tears and sweat from my face.

"There's nothing more for you here. Margaret will take you home." Margaret, or Maggie as she seemed to prefer, walked in the door behind her. She held an armful of fresh clothing.

"Well Miss Hybrid, let's get you all changed up so we can go." She held out the items to me. "We wouldn't want to return you to your lover boy smelling like an outhouse."

"So I just go home and pretend as though nothing ever happened?" I questioned again.

"Well, if it makes you feel any better, I will be hanging around for a bit." She smiled and threw the clothing at me after I'd hesitated in taking them.

"That's just great." Maggie seemed to appreciate the dripping tones of sarcasm.

As I walked by the old witch to follow Maggie, she grabbed my arm and whispered her warning in my ear. "We will keep an eye on you and if you mess up, trust and believe that we will come after you."

CHAPTER 25

"*I* thought you said you were alright." I looked him over and shook my head. Of course, he'd lied to me, anything to protect me. What was wrong with men that they thought something like that was necessary?

Rhys was lying on the couch. His leg wrapped in sloppy bandages that barely covered the large gash on his shin. At least the wound was no longer bleeding, but it still looked bad.

"What are you doing here? What happened?" He tried to get up and come to me but struggled to hold his own weight and fell back onto the couch.

"They let me go. Apparently the spirits found me worthy of continuing to live my life." I smiled and was happy to see the moment of relief on his face. Another wave of concern replaced the flash of happiness.

"What did they do to you?" He frowned. "You look sick."

"I look sick?" I laughed and deflected his question. "You're the one who can barely stand and yet I'm the one you're worried about. Priorities, Rhys. Priorities."

"I guess you're right." He laughed and then settled onto the couch. The look he gave me warmed my heart and lifted my spirit. To have someone so happy just to know that I was alive and well brought me a personal sense of joy.

"Here, let me help." I knelt in front of him and held my palms above his injured leg.

The necklace that hung against my chest vibrated as the power in my stone radiated to me. It moved in through my chest, passed through my arms and out of my hands. With a soft pink glow, my magic healed Rhys.

"Well, that's new." He smiled as he moved his leg without pain. "How did you learn to do that?" He stood and bounced around.

"I don't know, just instinct." I shrugged as I too got back to my feet.

"Well, isn't this just a beautiful moment? Gag me!" Maggie clapped her hands before she plopped down on the sofa, nearly crushing the leg I had just healed as she pushed past Rhys. "Now that you're all better, think you can whip us up something good to eat? I'm starved!"

"What the hell?" He looked between the two of us and waited for an answer.

"Maggie is the name. I don't think she made formal introductions during my first visit." She pointed at me. "This one is a real slacker in the manners department."

"What is she doing here?" Rhys looked at me for an answer.

Maggie's sarcastic sense of humor would only aggravate him more. It was already obvious that he wanted to give the girl a swift kick to the ass and send her out the door.

"The coven assigned her to monitor me for a while. I didn't think that meant she would have to bunk with us as well." I turned my gaze to Maggie, who just shrugged her shoulders and settled deeper into his couch.

"And what should I do? Would you have me pay for a hotel?" She asked with wide eyes, feigning hurt.

As if her coven wouldn't foot the bill, either with cash or magical deception. There was much more to her wanting to stay with us.

"I don't care what you do, you're not staying here." Rhys pointed to the door, a sign that it was time for her to leave.

"Look, how about I give you two a bit of privacy to sort things out?" Maggie stood from the couch and skipped to the door. "I'll be home for dinner, Pops." She laughed and the sound of her giggle was cut off when Rhys threw a ball of air that slammed the door behind her.

"That girl has a serious personality disorder." I couldn't help but to laugh. It was as if she flipped an internal switch and suddenly the bad ass who nearly broke Rhys' leg was a silly little kid.

"What is this about, Syrinada?" Rhys paced the floor. "We need to leave before she gets back."

"And go where? She'll find us; it's beyond our control now. The ancestral witch spirits have made it so." I shrugged.

I accepted her presence. What else was there to do? Could a person ever really outrun a ghost? Alderic had done it, or so it seemed, but what chances would I have?

"The ancestors?" Rhys paused in shock. "They actually called on them?"

"Yes, they summoned them, tortured me and made me drink this disgusting tea that made me vomit while they interrogated me. I guess my answers, my spirit or whatever, proved that I was worth the risk. This, of course, pissed off some of the witch elders, but they wouldn't touch me after the ancestors told them not to. They're afraid of the consequences. They did, however, assign little miss split personality," I nodded to the door, which Maggie had just used to leave, "to watch me until further notice."

"I don't want her here." He repeated his earlier sentiment, but in fewer words.

"Yeah, neither do I, but it's better than running and hiding. At least we know they won't be trying to kill me, if I don't slip up, that is."

"Great." My attempted joke fell flat on the ears of Rhys, who seemed lost in his own thoughts. He looked as if he was calculating some problem that only he was aware of.

"Who knows, it may be fun to have her around." I nudged his shoulder. "She'll obviously be a great source of entertainment."

"That's what the television is for." He smirked. It was small, but it was better than his previous frown. He sighed and with a serious expression said, "Please never do that again."

"Excuse me?" Our eyes locked. Though we were only a foot apart, Rhys looked at me like a canyon stood between us.

"Leave and not tell me where you are. Do you know how terrible I felt?" He inched forward, closing the space between our bodies.

"I'm sorry, Rhys, but I had to take care of it on my own. If you had come there, who knows how many people would have been hurt, including you. I couldn't risk that." As I spoke, he moved closer.

"Yet you risked your own life." He reached out and took my wrist into his hand. I swallowed the lump in my throat.

"Who better to put it on the line?" I smiled nervously. What was he thinking? What would he do? My heart raced as he stared at me.

Arms wrapped around me as he pulled me into him. "I'm serious. I can't lose you. You know that, don't you?" He leaned back so that I could see his face.

"Yes." My gaze traveled up his chest, over his face, to find eyes that turned my core to mush. He meant what he said, in more ways than I'd previously believed.

"Never again, promise me." He tightened his hold on me and I gasped.

It felt so good to be in his arms, to be so close to him. If he never let me go, I would have been completely happy in my existence.

"I promise." The vow came without hesitation. Unlike the last time I was asked to make a promise, there was no internal repulsion to the idea. I was ready to commit to Rhys and give him my companionship and my loyalty. My heart warmed with the realization of what that meant.

He lowered his lips to mine, and for the first time, we kissed. The world frozen in a moment, and I felt my body melt into his. This was it. This was that love that people dreamed about. When he kissed me, I felt nothing but love. It was so much more than the lust that lingered on the lips of those before him.

It wasn't the sex driven eagerness to rip away my clothes and taste more than just my lips and tongue. I felt completely and totally loved, and for the first time in my life, it was reciprocated. This man was mine; he was totally and completely mine, and I was ready to give everything I had to him.

"Rhys," I said his name in a breathy whisper.

"Yes?" His throaty response excited me more.

"Do that again." I smiled wholly and the siren inside of me stirred.

He laughed. "Gladly." The second kiss was just as good as the first and so were the third and the fourth.

His kisses remained just as sweet as they began as his lips moved from mine. Soft pecks touched my chin, jaw, neck, and shoulder. My head fell back as the soft moan escaped me.

"Rhys," I said his name softly.

"Yes, Syrinada." he responded, and my stomach squeezed.

I moaned again.

"Are you okay?" he stopped and looked me in my eyes. "I can stop."

"No," I caught my breath. "Please, don't."

Staring into his eyes, the deeps pools of chestnut, I knew this was the moment. This wasn't for healing or feeding my siren. It was for us. The next step in our relationship and it felt natural.

He lifted me from my feet and carried me into the bedroom, kissing me just as gently as before.

I felt the energy of the plants the moment we entered the room, and my body tingled as I pulled that to me. The new bamboo provided the same intoxicating effect as the others. Rhys laid me on the bed and stood in front of me.

He removed his clothes, and I watched as he presented himself to me. My eyes traveled the length of his body, toned from hours of training, and I smiled at the part of him I hadn't yet seen.

"Happy with what you see?" he chuckled at my expression.

"Yes, I am." I bit my lip as my body hummed.

I got up from the bed, pushed him down on it, and returned the favor. Seductively, I stripped, watching him closely as I peeled each layer away from my skin.

"Happy with what you see?" I licked my lips as his dick stiffened with his erection.

"Hell yeah." Rhys groaned.

"Stroke it." I ordered.

"What?" He asked as if confused by command.

"Your dick, stroke it. I want to watch." I requested again.

"Okay," he smiled and did as I asked. His eyes locked on me.

My pussy tightened with the sight of his hand moving across the length of his shaft. I couldn't help but to touch myself as well. I stood in front of him, massaging my clit with my fingertips as he continued to pleasure himself.

"I can't take this anymore." He lifted from the bed, grabbed my arm, and pulled me back down with him and I giggled like a child.

His lips muffled my laughter. And when his fingers replaced my own, that laughter turned to moans of pleasure.

"I want you." he whispered.

"You don't see me going anywhere." I responded with a wink.

Gently, he positioned himself on top of me. Rhys looked me in the eye as he slowly entered me, allowing me to experience every inch of him until he could go no further. He didn't move.

Instead, he kissed me, peppering my lips, chin, and neck with sweet touches until I couldn't take it anymore.

"Please." I spoke.

"What would you like?" He asked.

"Make love to me Rhys." I didn't expect the words, but that was my truth. I didn't want to be fucked, I wanted something sweeter, genuine. What I wanted was to feel his desire, his love, and for him to know that I felt the same way.

He smiled, eyes light with the love he felt for me, and Rhys did what I asked. He made love to me. Sweet, sensual love. And by the time he finished with me, I'd sung my siren song multiple times.

CHAPTER 26

"*I*s it safe to return?" Maggie poked her head in through the broken front door and looked around inside of the apartment.

After a few hours in bed, we got up and worked on getting the place in order. There wasn't much we could fix but we managed to clean up most of the damage. Our unwanted guest's first visit had left the living room completely wrecked.

"Yes, come in." I smiled at her and she raised a brow. What could I say? It was difficult to be sullen when I felt so utterly happy inside.

"I see you've tidied up the place. That's good because it was a mess in here!" She winked and all I could do was shake my head.

Rhys mumbled beneath his breath as he headed back into the kitchen.

"Welcome back." I continued sweeping the floor.

"Something smells wonderful!" she squealed as she once again plopped down onto the couch and offered no help in finishing the project.

"Yes, Rhys is an excellent cook." I complimented him loud enough for him to hear.

"I hope he made enough for me." Maggie responded even louder, which got an agitated grunt from the cook.

"I'm sure there'll be plenty." I nodded confidently. Rhys had a terrible habit of making meals large enough to feed a crew of men and not just the two of us. "So, tell me how this is supposed to work. How long are you going to be tagging along with me?"

"They didn't tell me all that. To be honest, they were upset that they had to let you walk out of there. I wouldn't be surprised if I became your buddy indefinitely." She shrugged as if it made no difference to her either way.

Her response to the new almost made me believe Maggie was looking forward to hanging around. It also brought up the question of why she was suddenly so comfortable being near me.

"You're okay with that? Having to stay by the side of a woman you were so eager to kill just a few days ago doesn't bother you?" I stopped sweeping the floor and gave her my full attention.

"Nope. I do what the assignment calls for. Besides, I wasn't going to kill you. It was all for show, to kinda shake you up a bit." She looked to see if Rhys had come from the kitchen. He hadn't, but she still lowered her voice.

"Look, I just do what I'm told. But to be honest, I think it's a crappy hand you've been dealt. I'm glad those spirits saw the better side of you. I've been watching you for a while now, since right before you left Chicago and went to New Orleans, which was a ballsy move, by the way.

"Yeah, you struggled, but you tried to do better. There have been other sirens who just went completely bat shit crazy and started killing every man that crossed their path." She shook her head as she remembered what she witnessed my counterparts do.

"You aren't like the rest of them, and they should have never treated you like you were. Unfortunately, no matter what I report back, they make their own decisions. That is, until the higher powers step in."

"So there are others like me?" I joined her on the couch. Newly intrigued by what information she could give me.

Maggie was another well of knowledge that I could now tap into. Having her around would prove to benefit me.

"Yes, a few. Not the same combination, but other hybrids exist. These magical folk like to pretend that they never sinned, but they did, and it turned out so bad. Now they're trying to clean up the mess. Before, when things got messy, they never summoned the spirits. They made their own verdicts and it led to hell on earth and a big ass whooping from the ancestors.

Now, they have to call them. They went around chopping down any anomaly they came across until Ebon appeared and cast their judgment. If they killed anyone else without first allowing the ancestors to cast judgment, our elders would suffer."

"I see." That must have been why the old woman was so upset. She didn't want the spirits to come. They forced her to call them; they took away her power and her authority.

"Food is ready," Rhys announced as he placed two plates on the table. He sat down with one plate in front of him and indicated that the other was for me.

"Aw, no service for a lady?" Maggie stood from the couch and walked to stand over Rhys and eye the food on his plate. She took a deep inhale and moaned. "Oh, my goodness, that smells delicious!"

"You can help yourself. I'm sure you can find the kitchen." He ate his food and ignored the kisses she blew in his direction before dancing off towards the kitchen.

I laughed and took my place next to him. "You're really going to make her suffer, huh?"

"Hey, she busted my favorite lamp and cracked the screen on the TV with her little show; she can get her own food." He bit down into the dinner roll and smiled around the mouthful of bread.

"I'll pay for the damage!" Maggie called from the kitchen.

"See, problem solved." I smiled and put a spoonful of food in my mouth. A moan of appreciation like Maggie's came from me, and he grinned again.

"Yeah, right?" He grunted.

"Aren't we just the happy little trio?" She returned from the kitchen and sat down opposite me and to the left of Rhys, who raised an eyebrow in her direction but kept eating.

"You're seriously going to stick around?" He finally asked after a long pause. Maggie and I were too busy eating to be bothered by conversation.

"Yes, I am. It would be great for all of us if you would just accept it, big guy." She smacked him on the shoulder but quickly removed her hand when he looked at it. The enormous grin that spread across her face told me we were in for a fun time.

Rhys and I shared a bed that night while Maggie took over the pullout couch in the front. We'd debated her sharing a bed with me, but Rhys didn't trust her enough for that. He insisted we stay together. Maggie insinuated he had other things in mind, but nothing happened.

We talked a bit, and I fell asleep with my head on his shoulder. Maggie stayed up watching a standup comedy on the cracked television. Every now and then, I would hear her laugh or talk back at the screen. The girl was even more opinionated when she was the only one in the room.

Waking up wasn't as peaceful of an experience. At four in the morning, before the sun rose, I opened my eyes to an angry Alderic standing at the foot of the bed. Dark eyes locked on me. He said nothing, but words weren't needed to express the hatred he felt for me.

The daughter he once claimed to love, and miss was now being crushed under the weight of his hatred. He held his hand out and my head hurt. A moment later, my tears ran in a crimson flow that stained the white sheet wrapped around me. I struggled and cried out for him to stop, but of course, he refused.

"What's wrong?" Rhys awakened and, of course, tried to help me, but before he could see him, Alderic knocked him across the room with a force of power that sent him flying from the bed to the floor.

"You betrayed me. My own flesh and blood and you walked away from me!" my father yelled. "If I can't have you by my side, there is no purpose for your existence." Then a bright light blinded me just before everything faded to black.

"Syrinada, please wake up!" Rhys called my name and shook my body. His hands clutched my shoulders as he tried to jolt me back to consciousness.

I sat up and looked at him. He was okay. Not injured or burned. A quick scan of the room told me we were alone. Nothing had happened. It was only a dream, no matter how real it felt. "What happened?"

"You were sleeping, you started screaming. Are you okay?" He looked at me closely, pulled me into his arms into a tight hug, and then looked me over again.

"Yes, I'm sorry. It was a bad dream." I took a deep breath. My limbs still felt heavy as if Alderic was still there and using his magic to crush me.

"What the hell was all that about?" Maggie spoke from the doorway.

"What are you doing in here?" Rhys turned on her as if she were the source of my nightmare.

"Making sure the all-powerful siren doesn't kill anybody. Otherwise known as doing my job, duh." She stepped further into the room and took her turn in examining the patient.

"How would she have killed someone?" Rhys stood and put a shirt on, as it became clear that Maggie wouldn't be leaving. Previously, he'd only worn a pair of shorts, which I hadn't complained about.

"Hell, if I know, no one really knows what she is capable of."

"I'm fine. You can both stop talking about me as if I'm not sitting right here."

"Sorry, so it was just a bad dream?" Maggie touched my forehead, and I pushed her hand away.

Yeah, I had accepted that she would be around, but that didn't mean she was invited into my personal space.

"Yeah, a really bad dream." I sighed. "Can we all just try to get some sleep?"

Four nights later and I was still having the same dream. Each time, the dream became more intense, and brutal. My father took his time in torturing me, and he tried over and over to get me to break and give in to what he wanted. Each time that I refused, he ended my life.

I sat up in a cold sweat, staring at the window.

"Again?" Rhys asked.

"Yes," I wiped my forehead.

"Syrinada. Please tell me, what is happening in the dream. What's wrong?"

"It's my father." I admitted and sighed. "I hate that I'm dreaming about him. Maybe I miss him. But I hate that man. How could I still want to see him?

"What exactly happens in the dream?"

"I see him, hovering over the bed. He asks me to return to him. I say no, and then he," I could say it.

"He what?"

"He kills me," I blurted out. "He hurts you and he kills me."

"Oh, my god." Rhys stood from the bed.

"What's wrong?" I watched as he paced the floor for a moment.

"Those aren't just dreams Syrinada." Rhys looked at me with worried eyes. "I think Alderic is trying to find you and the dreams are weakening your defenses against him."

"What do you mean?" How could a dream weaken me?

"I mean, if it continues, eventually he'll find you. Hell, that's if he doesn't already know where you are."

"Okay, another early morning." Maggie appeared in the doorway, yawning. "Assuming another bad dream."

She stretched her arms above her head, but when she caught out worried expressions, she paused. "Wait, what happened?"

"Alderic has been channeling Syrinada. That's why she keeps having those dreams."

"What?" she looked at me. "How long has this been going on?"

"Since you got here." Rhys pointed.

"Don't do that." I pleaded.

"Yeah, I'm not the one who was buddy-buddy with the reject warlock, you were." Maggie pointed her finger at him. "He probably has a magical GPS implanted in your ass!"

"Enough!" I barked. "None of this is helpful. What the hell are we supposed to do now?"

"Well, if this continues, by the time Alderic gets to you, you won't be able to defend yourself." Rhys answered me.

"Yeah, and judging by the sad state of the plants in here," she pointed to the line of plant life along the wall, "you're already pretty damn weak."

I swallowed the knot in my throat as I realized I'd been taking more from them to make myself feel better, but not cycling the energy back to them.

"We need to go back to New Orleans." Rhys started packing a bag. It was six in the morning and the sun had only peeked into the sky.

"Why?" I stood from the bed. "The last time I was in New Orleans, everything went to shit fast. How could returning there be a good idea?"

"My mother is there." Rhys rubbed my shoulders. "She can help us."

"Won't he just be able to find us if we are all out in the open?" Maggie pointed out the obvious flaw in the plan Rhys was putting forward.

"Well, we're under a damn cloak now and look at what he is doing to her!" He continued throwing items into the bag, which I took from him. If we were going to pack to leave, we would take things we needed. Nine pairs of socks and one pair of underwear wouldn't work. "Eventually, he will find her regardless. The best thing we can do is to get her somewhere where she can be protected."

"True." Maggie dropped her head, and they both looked at me.

Ultimately, it was my decision to stay or go. Really, what choice did I have? I could be hardheaded and stay, which would mean risking the lives of yet two more people I cared about. That wasn't something I was willing to do. Besides, I'd made a promise to the witch ancestors and if I had to choose which entity would be coming for me, it sure as hell wouldn't be a trio of century old dead witches. No, thank you!

"Fine, let's go. Whatever it takes to get this to stop. I will get ready to go." Rhys smiled, Maggie sighed, and I headed for the bathroom. I needed a long bath and a stiff drink.

CONTINUE
THE
STORY

ABOUT THE AUTHOR

Born and raised in Chicago, IL, writing has always been a passion for Jessica Cage. She dabbles in artistic creations of all sorts but at the end of the day, it's the pen that her hand itches to hold. Jessica had never considered following her dream to be a writer because she was told far too often "there is no money in writing." so she chose the path most often traveled. During pregnancy she asked herself an important question. How would she be able to inspire her unborn son to follow his dreams and reach for the stars, if she never had the guts to do it herself? Jessica decided to take a risk and unleash the plethora of characters and their crazy adventurous worlds that had previously existed only in her mind, into the realm of readers. She did this with hopes to inspire not only her son but herself. Inviting the world to tag along on her journey to become the writer she has always wanted to be. She hopes to continue writing and bringing her signature caged fantasies to readers everywhere.

Connect with Jessica and visit her website: www.jessicacage .com